Everyday Life

Everyday Life
AC Pritts

ISBN-13: 9781703764321

Printed and bound in the United States of America

Published by KDP Direct Publishing
www.kdp.amazon.com

Dedication

This is presented as a work of fiction. The dedication of this book is to my Liebchen, my Honey Bear, my Love Bug, my parents and you the reader.

Table of Contents

Foreword

Life is hard! And even though we may not be of this world, we certainly are in it. Where the choice lies is whether we allow the struggles, trauma, and challenges to defeat us or to transform us. My bias is that I believe that god invites us in every moment of our everyday life to become more and more the Beloved Child of god he intends us to be. My prayer is that journeying with Jaime in this book you too may be encouraged to know the "Bigness" of God.

The Rev. Don C. Youse, Jr.

Emmanuel Episcopal Church

Preface

It's time for a book that sheds light on everyday life's circumstances from a different point of view. Life is hard and if anyone tells you otherwise it is false. Who among us lives in utopia? Perfect we are not, and never will be, however we have something to soften sorrows' blow. The recollection to come to the conclusion that we are stronger than the afflictions we may face. The connections and feelings of love we share with one another. It helps us, it shapes us, it changes us. We yearn for it, thrive on it, and can become our very best because of it. Sorrow and love are universal, knowing no barriers to race, creed, wealth, or age. This book is dedicated to anyone who has experienced the woes of sorrow. This book cannot change your life, but can create opportunities, providing a window if you will, into thoughts and feelings of your own everyday life.

1971

I remembered too much detail – details, I contradict them not. Some of the words that came out of my mouth infuriated me, at times to no end as they fell on death ears. Let me explain, just let me explain. I could recall but others chose not to remember and still others would not want to hear. They would dismiss it as pure nonsense, an imagination of the mind if they did listen. It may have been too much for the sensitive hearts or maybe they just didn't care. But I simply wanted to be heard, whatever it was, nonsense or not, I would tell the tales that should have been heard then.

Suzie Nook was a blue eyed, attractive woman who I sometimes called my blue-eyed soul because of her captivating steel blue eyes. Suzie was a natural beauty with red hair, a strong – willed woman, my blue-eyed soul, yet a survivor -- or maybe not. I will leave that up to you the reader to decide. Yes, I could be quite sarcastic during those times. Suzie's impact and lack of concern for my sorrow could really pack a punch. Poor thing, Suzie, she only knew what she had learned.

I was a small child at the time, I was a pretty little thing with auburn color hair and big dark brown eyes. Nestled in the arms of my molester from the tender age of three. I had served a six-year sentence with that. And was eight years old at the time when Suzie told her tale. The chocolate- donut man made his presence known that day by yelling; *chocolate donuts, chocolate donuts*, as he stood at the outside of the kitchen door. After hearing his deep low voice that seemed to echo through the opened kitchen windows, I felt afraid. How hearing his voice haunted me. I had hoped he would just go away. I thought no one heard the fear in my voice as I had yelled out, *Leave the donuts at the door, no one wants you here*! At that time some of them who were there just chuckled when I tried warning them of the danger that stood at the kitchen door. And at times my warnings were not spoken, yet my actions spoke volumes then, that anyone could have seen, if only they cared enough to notice. But I noticed the empty look there in his eyes - could they not see – like a cloud without rain in it on a rainy day. Chocolate donuts, only one for me - it was always only one - yet I endured ten times more. No, no one had seen through that smile on his face and the evil intent in those eyes of his, no, only me!

"Oh, do let him in, Jamie, Jamie Jederman, the donut- man, has my chocolate donuts, goodies for me!" Suzie said in a soft but authoritative tone of voice. So, I opened the kitchen door! I kept my head down walking toward the door, dragging my feet along the way, they felt heavy like lead to me. Tugging hard to open the tightly sealed door as I was a thin child and not very strong. I was focusing on the whoosh sound that came after the seal between the door and its hinge came apart, then felt the air on my body that rushed in. Sadly, the air brought with it the smell of the donut-man too. His sweat and musk cologne hung there in the air and I imagined it laid my body. I couldn't even smell the freshly baked donuts; I didn't think anyone could until the box of donuts would be opened. He stepped into the kitchen but he could not stay that time too many people around, his plans for me had gone astray. I was saved. A quick

"Hello, Jamie," the donut - man uttered.

"Goodbye, Jamie,"

he gave me with an irritating smug grin on his face. He told Suzie, and all that were there who were listening, that he could not stay. That he would come back and stay later when company wasn't around besides, he just wanted to drop off Suzie's donuts. Donuts, it was always only one for me as he was closing the door, I thought. I gave him a sarcastic smirk, and thought I should be able to get two donuts then. I pushed the door closed almost hitting the back of his boot, I had wished I did! It was 1971 that summer day in Pittsburgh Pennsylvania. I had listened to some of the adults talk about a park opening and it sounded like fun; that was before I heard the donut-man outside the kitchen door. I was always around the adults it seemed, not much time to play for me. And I was there when Suzie, my blue-eyed soul, told her petrifying tale of how her uncle killed a chicken. Suzie and I were in the company of four to six of her slightly drunken friends there in the kitchen. I had just pushed the kitchen door closed on Suzie's favorite donut – man! Her friends would leave the kitchen at times to use the only bathroom upstairs, which could cause quite a heavy traffic flow of people in and out of the old looking kitchen. A yield sign would have been useful that day to slow and yield the right away to the incoming people. Into the sometime smoked filled old kitchen, though some of the smoke had made its way out of the windows, a stink like cigarettes and whiskey, came the clinking sounds of ice cubes as they dropped into their glasses with the sound of 'Poison" as they called it, being poured into their glasses. As the men and women's laughter and loud talking filled the room, it all reminded me of Jack's Bar. How I could even pick up on the different types of smells they had as I walked by Suzie's friends. There were unrinsed dishes in the sink and the opened half- empty box of donuts was on the sink counter. I was right, I could smell them since the box was open. I was eating a donut, they were all cake donuts with chocolate icing, and it was good. I would swoosh the icing around in my mouth. I had thought there was something good about the donut- man, the donut was good.

The walls were yellow in the kitchen with burnt orange painted wooden wainscoting and the upper and lower shutters on the three kitchen windows were all in the open position, and a warm sweet-smelling summer breeze would blow in at times, a welcomed treat. I often stared at the walls and thought about other things when I got bored.

"I've got, something to say it's been on my mind for a long time," Suzie said.

Suzie had paused for a moment to clear her cracked voice.

"Yeah, my uncle was nude!" She informed us, her face turned pale and her steel blue eyes grew wider and those in the kitchen at the time saw her heart beat pound through her neck, I did too. They became quiet, then there was a whimpering sound that caught the ear, Suzie was crying. Her blue eyes looked so blue, the tears seemed to hang there at Suzie's pupil before they fell, and rested high on her high cheek bone just below her blue eyes. Then she repeated the word "Nude" as she wiped her tears away. And all who were there then listened for what Suzie would say next. They watched her with their bloodshot eyes, I watched too. I stood in the corner by the window, I was always there during those times, unless the donut – man arrived first, then I would join in later, in that corner out- of -sight -out -of - mind. I felt breathless. I felt the pounding of my heart and I was on pins and needles with that second donut in my left hand. . . I wasn't bored. All these emotions I was experiencing, all because I heard the nude and Suzie was crying. The smoke had cleared from the kitchen, the breeze carried in the fragrance of honeysuckle from the plants that were in the side garden. I heard one more glass of "poison" being poured before Suzie spoke; yet, that time she spoke in a childlike voice.

Suzie explained, "Yeah, my uncle was nude when he killed that chicken in my Grandma's kitchen right in front of me! He wielded it around, laughing with such a strange look on his face- one I never had seen before. He jerked that chicken back and forth at me and his nude body at me too. He plucked at its feathers that bird was flapping its wings about, squawking, clucking feathers flowed in the air. And when my uncle went to that old chopping block to chop its head off, our eyes made contact that bird and mine; right before the chop! As if, that bird was pleading to me for help! Stupid stinky bird, it was a hard-solid sound, one swift hit then it was all over for that bird! Its blood seemed like it was squirting everywhere. My uncle seemed to be covered in blood; he thrusted that thing at me and his male parts at me too. His eyes were glistening and my eyes pleaded with him for mercy. I screamed in horror and was crying as he gave chase, chasing me around Grandma's kitchen. I thought if only Grandma was home this wouldn't be happening. I wished my Daddy would come bursting into the kitchen and save me! I asked him to stop, yet, my request only encouraged him more as he began to grunt and groan- my ears went deaf I couldn't hear a sound anymore! He had caught me hitting me with that thing, its pulsating warm blood seemed to cover me. Then it was cold, it was on my arms, then rolled down from my arms dripping off my elbows as I used my arms as a shield. And blood splashed landing on my face, on my budding breasts because my yellow sundress was ripped. We then had chicken for dinner that night!"

Suzie's steel blue eyes stared a vacant stare. It was like Suzie wasn't there anymore – petrified! I cried in silence for Suzie not to disturb the quietness that had consumed the room as I sat there on the kitchen floor in the corner. And as the tears rolled down my face, I looked at the yellow wall and my imagination carried me away.

◊

I remembered how my brother James had hated me so.

"I hate you; Jamie I always have and I always will until the day I die!" James informed me with such rage in his voice and a look of disgust on his face. I had told him I loved him and always would, he was my brother; and then I hung my head low.

"If, you say that one more time, I'm going to punch you in the face!" James shouted.

I never said it again.

We were both the babies of the family, seventeen months apart in age. He was the youngest of the boys and I was the youngest of the girls, and the baby of them all. Maybe, that was why he hated me, I thought, because I cut into his baby time with Mom and Daddy. Maybe, it was because I was Daddy's little girl and of course you know could do no wrong. But whatever it was that angered him so, torn me apart at times then or at least it felt like it to me.

It was the simplest things, really, that I done to annoy him, merely walking past him. I got a punch to the face and a blow to the guts. Poor thing, I laid there on the cold hard hardwood floor in the front hallway of our Victorian house grasping for air, moaning a strong painful moan. While James stood over me in an arrogant rough stance and made fun of me at my expense, I closed my eyes; listening to his devilish laugh as I caught my breath. And with a quick kick to my side from James, my beating was over. I then heard his footsteps as he ran off.

I got back on my feet by pressing my back against the sky-blue hall wall, pushing up with my legs in an upward sliding motion. While, I was cupping my mouth with my left hand in my attempt to catch my blood. Once on my feet I held my head back for the bitter iron taste of blood to flow down the back of my throat. That was done to avoid any more blood from getting on my light blue blouse. Then glancing downward with my eyes, I noticed the blood flowing on the old hardwood floor, it had settled in place and began to seep into the cracks. My heart began to race but not for the sight of blood, that was all-to-familiar to me. It was due to fear because of the mess I had made on my light blue blouse as well as the mess on the floor.

The pain was no more, fright had taken its place and I was on pins and needles as I made my way carefully towards the kitchen. I had a mission; I had to stop the bleeding, clean the floor, and at the very least soak that blouse before Mom made her descent from her bedroom to finish the day's wash (worsh).

I struggled while turning the kitchen sink cold water spicket on with my trembling right hand placing the other trembling hand in the then steady stream of cold water. The water filled up in the palm of my hand then flowed over the side and through my bloody fingers, as the water took on a reddish hue. I worshed the blood stains from the back of my hand and watched as the droplets of my blood fell into the stream of water, then in a swirl fashion down the drain it went. I pushed my shoulder length hair back several times then I cried just a little; my tears were no longer mine they made their way down the drain too. I had been mesmerized by the cascading water, and the ticking sounds of the rooster clock that hung on the yellow kitchen wall between the two shuttled windows above the table. Then I felt a sadness fall over me due to the countless times at the kitchen sink under those same circumstances. Yet, I was thankful there were no dishes in the sink, Ha-Ha! A quick glance for the time and I hurried my task along applying pressure to my bleeding, swollen lower lip with some paper towel stopping the bleeding, then a quick clean-up of the sink area and I was on my way with paper towel in hand back to the scene of the crime.

I had made it there just in time wiping what I could see of my blood off the floor then checking the wall, it was good. I could see Mom, she stood at the top of the steps her hourglass silhouette was cast on the hallway wall from the sun light that came from her bedroom window and through the open bedroom door. I was almost done; I felt a sense of accomplishment, breathing a sigh of relief and made my way back towards the kitchen to the basement door right outside the kitchen in the hall. Then down the step I went taking the blouse off as I went almost falling down the step but didn't care because Mom was on her way. I reached the worsh (wash) area of the basement, stopped up the stationary sink, turned the cold water on, threw that blouse in the water grabbing the soap and began to scrub that blouse. Then I let it soak while I grabbed an old t-shirt from the table, putting it on.

"Hey, Jamie, are you down there!" Mom yelled.

I yelled back and told her yes, that I was worshing clothes and then hurried pulling the drain stopper to let the water drain and placing that blouse in the ringer worsher with some like colored clothes and turning it on. I was enjoying the quick moving whoosh sounds of the clothes being worshed, but I had grown tired of playing the avoidance game, yet it had worked. It kept me out of trouble in the past and I was hoping it would work out this time too. Although, it would have been nice to explain what had happened without getting into any more trouble. Mom and my sister Jennifer had joined me in the basement to finish that day's warsh. I thought how clever I was but had forgotten what it was I wanted done at the time James beat me up in the hall. I had to be clever to keep my face in the shadow spots of the dimly lit warsh area with its one overhead pull string light bulb. I would remain in the shadow so Jennifer or Mom couldn't see my swollen lower lip. If it had been seen, it would have spelled double trouble for me from Mom and James in the end. How great I thought it would have been if I could have just been able to explain things and that it would be okay in the end, like the family I watched on the T.V. But no, besides, Mom doted on the boys. Jennifer handed me a full basket of clothes, adding my blouse to the top of the basket to be hung up on the outside clothes line and off I went.

I thought about James as I was walking up the basement step; I knew I would have to be around him at dinner time but thought he was probably gone bike riding by then, it was a sunny summer day that day. I placed the clothes basket on the ground then reaching into the clothe pin bag on the line I took out two clothe pins with that blouse in the other hand and there he was; James! He had just jumped on his red bike. I thought he had waited around to take a look at his handy work. He looked at my face, my mouth, then he was laughing as I hang that damn light blue blouse up on the line. Laugh it up punk boy, I thought as I continued at my task, attempting to shield my face with each piece of clothing I hung.

"Nice, fat lip you got there Jamie!" James reminded me, he then stretched out his arm towards me waving his hand side-to-side at me.

"Goodbye, see you and that fat lip I gave you later!' He informed me. I took a moment to stare at him watching him ride away. And in that moment, I found myself physically exhausted and mentally drained, it had been a long day and it was close to noon. After I hung the last shirt up, I took a needed break. I sat down on the glider in the yard admiring that damn light blue blouse of mine, it looked good! I enjoyed hearing the birds chirping, feeling the warmth of the day's sun on my tired sore body. I thanked God for the opportunity to rest, it seemed like things worked out for the best and I was calm, thanks to God. Then I closed my eyes to relax and listened to the sounds and took in the smells of the goodness of summer and thought about Suzie.

◊

Chicken dinner, I thought, as I sat in the kitchen corner watching Suzie. She had picked up her drink in a robot-like way and drank. I thought, my God, as tears streamed down my face, what a horrible crazy uncle Suzie had, all that blood; I hated chicken. Brave Suzie, she told everyone about what happen to her, maybe it was my turn to tell what had happen to me. Yeah, but what about my blue-eyed soul, someone should say something. Okay, on the count of three: one, two ... I opened my mouth to speak and a loud chaotic laughter erupted; its sound filled the kitchen; it was all I could hear. Suzie's laugh was the loudest.

"Yeah, those were the days, right Suzie? Ha-Ha- those were the day!" Ajax declared in a deep raspy voice. I didn't find it funny at all; I had my ears covered, shook my head, frowning at them all, frowning at Ajax then kept my eyes on Suzie. She wasn't laughing anymore, I stared angrily for a moment at Ajax who was standing in the center of the kitchen which made sense to me; he always liked to be the center of attention. He then was walking towards the bench and sat down close to Suzie whose chair was at the head of the table next to the sink. I remained in my corner diagonal to Suzie. Ajax was the type of guy that liked to, as he would say, *leave them laughing*; he thought it was better than sorrow-- he was right about that. He leaned in with that tall lanky body of his and whispered something in Suzie's right ear, attempting to use his quick-witted charm and good looks on her to help change her mood, I thought. I guessed he called it clearing the air, hence his nick name. But all I knew was my blue-eyed soul wasn't laughing and sat motionless with her eyes low and all eyes were on her. Ajax had sat back in his seat.

An attractive, disheveled looking woman got up from her chair opposite end of Suzie. She walked over to Suzie, attempting to adjust her pink top, smoothing her brown hair back while tugging at her multicolor skirt that formed to her pear-shaped body, her attempted to enhance her appearance I imagined. She then used her elbow, nudging Suzie back around; Suzie glare up at the woman, then watched her as she poured them both drinks placing her left hand on Suzie's shoulder. The woman used her blood shot hazel eyes to draw the others attention to her instead of on Suzie. She and the others all raised their glasses high.

"To Suzie!" She praised and the others followed suit like a domino effect and then they all drank. Suzie drank once more! Several quiet, yet sobering conversations about random things then took place. Suzie's eyes fell on me, her eyes looked as though she was deep in thought.

Poor little Jamie, her donut on the floor, she looked like someone hit her in the gut -knocking the breath out of her, so drained of life--was this all for me? Suzie must have thought, then laughed out loud, Ajax chimed in.

"There it is, that's what I like to hear, Suzie!" Ajax joked. Suzie smiled slightly, hitting the table with her right palm of her hand and made herself another Orange Crush pop and Windsor Canadian whisky drink. She motioned to me, wiggling her right hand at me, then told me to clean up that mess I'd made from the donut which was on the floor.

"When, you're done with that, Jamie, make yourself useful and do those dishes," Suzie demanded. I knew she felt better; I could see it in those eyes of her, she didn't have to say a word. I told her okay, but I was trembling inside while I was walking over to the sink and got the trash can and the dust pan. I picked up that second donut, looked at it, shoving it deep down in to the trash. Then I used the side of my hand to gather the crumbs onto the dust pan still horrified about what I heard. I placed the trash can and the dust pan back in their place beside the sink, opposite side of Suzie, right under the light blue phone that hung on the wall, and started on those dishes. I found myself becoming unaware of the people around me and their sound of their voice faded and I thought back to my brother James.

◊

It was dinner time, there were three dining tables in that old Victorian house. The dining room table was an Antique Mahogany Dining Set that belonged my maternal Grandmother. It could seat eight people once Mom put in the table leaf to extent it. Mom thought that it was perfect for the dining room, it complemented the off-white marble mantelpiece with fireplace along with the two large natural wood shuttered windows on the opposite wall of the mantel. It was quite beautiful, and it was my job to dust the table and chairs too. There was also a small kitchen table that would sometimes be placed in the kitchen alongside the corner wall next to the window and refrigerator, or placed in the dining room during a given meal, depending on the type of company. Finally, James and I had sat at the heads of the four chaired, yellow painted, wooden small table. The other kids had graduated to the kitchen table.

That night the yellow table had been placed in the dining room, there was adult company, but I would see them after dinner. So, I felt like a prisoner, a captive audience as we sat there. My plated food was in front of me and I thanked the Lord for the food.

"Nice lip, wonder who gave you that- oh yeah that would be me, right Jamie?" James asked.

"Yeah, so funny," I replied, then thought, "jag-off."

"Let's see, what do I want from Jamie's plate, I meant my plate," James said helping himself to the chicken leg, I didn't eat the foul-smelling bird anyway. Gobble it up, James, I thought. He was doing me a favor, imagine that, if only he knew. He threw his carrots on my plate smashing some of them between his index finger and thumb then walking his index and middle fingers through my mashed potatoes stopped only when he had hit a hot spot. However, I didn't care. I kept my big dark brown eyes on his right stretched out arm, his hand balled in a fist close to his head and was in the ready to strike position.

"Okay, Jamie you can eat, enjoy your food big lip," He ordered, glaring at me with those beautiful but evil hazel eyes of his with that crazy smirk on his face. He dared me to make a sound so that the mighty hammer like fist of his could come down and hit its target... me. So, I ate whether I liked it or not, and his arm slowly came down and he placed it to his side. Although, it was hard to eat with a swollen low lip with a large cut on the inside of the lip. James was laughing, he took much pleasure at my expense watching me while I took every painful burning bite- salt in an opened wound. Some of the food fell from my lower lip onto my t-shirt; it was then I remembered that I was on my way to change my blouse when James beat me up in the hall way. James clapped his hands.

"Good girl, make sure you eat it all," He demanded

Then he got up from the yellow chair that he was really too big to sit at any more due to his slightly husky size and then left the room. I stared down at my dining plate, looked at the leftovers and my mind wandered; my imagination kicked in.

◊

Fragmented broken off detached smashed pieces of my heart, woe always me I thought. I cried out for help and always no one there to help me. A protective shield was what I needed. I thought it would have kept me from harm. A smile was all I had that covered all that was beaten, molested and battered. I was leftovers too. And oh, what great lessons I had to live by. I often found myself in a state of wonder, wondering "why" and "what if" frame of mind.

Yet, I remained polite, for the most part, a giver and even told all my frightening ugly monster's goodnight and God bless.

The Lord's Pray & Hail Mary was said right before we all went to sleep in my house, and sometimes Raymond would stretch out the word "womb". Suzie would get so mad. She told Raymond not to stretch the womb, laughter had broken out, I'd laughed too, but I didn't get it. It was just nice to laugh and hear laughter I thought. Suzie would make us start the prayer over. When that would happen, my monsters were blessed twice, maybe that would do it, I had thought, or maybe armor would do. It was all weird to me, the behavior and events of the day only to pray at night. After the chaos – the destruction. I didn't understand this type of love, if this was love, I thought I didn't want any more of it.

◊

Armor, I recalled Mom had told me that her Dad had abandoned the family when she was just a little girl. We had been in the yard and had sat on the glider and Mom was in a talkative mood as we enjoyed the night summer air.

"Daddy left me; I thought he would come back to save me. Daddy would ride in on a white horse, a knight in his shining armor to rescue me, but he never did come back!" Mom said.

I had a puzzled look on my face and I had asked her why?

"I, don't know, Mommy said Daddy left because I was ugly, but I'm not. She hated me. She left too when I was ten and I had to live with my Grandma," Mom groaned.

I told Mom I loved her, but I must have been talking too low, she didn't say anything. I hung my head but still listened.

"Mommy came home from work one evening, my sister and I were setting the table, my mouth was watering and my stomach growled from smelling the goulash, very little meat. Grandma had cooked and I was so hungry. Mommy walked in the house at a fast pace, her high heels clicking on the tile floor, I'll never forget that sound, as she made her way to a back bedroom. She changed her clothes, packed a bag and came into the kitchen, handing Grandma some money. Then she took some of it back and told Grandma it was for the Nickelodeon Theatre. I didn't understand then. Grandma kept telling Mommy no, not to do it, still Mommy was walking on towards the front of the house to the front door but at a slower pace than before, bag in hand. We followed behind, I could recall thinking how pretty Mommy looked in her form-fitting dark blue dress, her hair in an updo. She had reached the front door, opened it wide and kept her hand on the door knob facing the three of us, then she told us not to wait up. Grandma called to her daughter, "Bertha!" Mom shuddered and I had no words.

"That, was a long movie- - Bertha was gone for sixteen years. I took care of my Grandma, my sister was out on her own then," She described in a sorrowful sounding voice. Mom kept her head down low; I couldn't see her eyes but imagined how sad they must have looked.

◊

It was late and I was done with those dishes. I said my "good night" and "God bless" to all who remained in the kitchen with Suzie. But I didn't care to turn the whole way around, I only looked to my right at Suzie. Then walked off only after she gave me the look to do so, and I was grateful for the permission. I was tired. I knew I didn't want to hear any more stories of any kind. I went to my room which was the attic of the house; I wept bitterly. And when I was done with that, I pushed my emotions, my sorrow's woes deep, deep down into what seemed like a bottomless pit in my gut, or maybe in my soul. And like that donut, I had shoved it deep into the trash, I gave up caring for myself, not caring anymore; at least that was the plan. And from then on, I wear a care giver's crown. I guessed it was always there; yet, I had decided to focus on others and to hell with myself. It was easier, no one seemed to care, so why should I. I was junk, but I was good at taking care of others and it gave me a sense of survival. I had good coping skills and it was better than armor. I had my imagination, and I prayed for a better, always prayed, for a better day. And time moved on. I wasn't eight years old anymore but a teenager.

1976

I remembered it was 1976; I was given a time out from my regularly scheduled everyday life, or at least I thought. After all those years of going to church, it finally paid off. All those years I thought, in my thirteen-year-old obscured mind while I was walking to church to attend the 10: 00 a.m. service. People were busy talking about the prices of food and gas, inflation, I was inflated with my sorrow's woes. I had prayed for God to save me but he never kept me safe from my monsters. I could recall one Saturday night- fun night - when I was six years old, fun for the "donut-man" then I had good old church in the morning. Right after I scrubbed that strong unpleasant odor from my body parts then it was off to church. It seemed like I could smell it even after I had bathed.

I had walked into church nervously wondering if anyone could smell me too or saw how dirty I was. I sat down on the back-church pew and received my normal looks from the adults. I prayed before I had gone to bed, in the morning, and when I saw the donut-man. I prayed for Suzie and James too. I prayed at church the longest, lit candles, and always nothing. And every Sunday morning I was given four quarters for the collection plate and had to walk pass the penny candy store- Uh just passed it. And during church service then, at collection time, I'd put all four quarters in the plate, all the times when I was younger, but not that day. Oh no, I was thirteen then, so I kept a quarter, I thought payment for my troubles.

After church I ran to the penny candy store and took my time picking out the best twenty-five pieces of penny candy from what seemed liked hundreds to select from. I enjoyed that candy, there were: fireballs, black cows, Swedish fish and so much more. I shared too. Kenny had seen me and ran across the street to reach me while tugging at the bit of brown hairs he had on his chin, he was cute and a typical skinny kid.

"Hi, church girl, what you got there?" Kenny asked in a crack sounding voice, then coughed clearing his throat for a stronger tone, because his voice was changing. I didn't answer. I shrugged my shoulders and kept on walking the eight blocks to my house.

"Candy, you've got candy, Jamie, I can smell it. Can I have some?" He asked.

"Sure", I had replied, but then had said "psych!"

You know it was like a trick -psych your mind- "psych".

"So, Jamie, where you get the money from to buy the candy, how much do you have?" He said.

I had told him that I found a quarter on the ground.

"Where, on the ground, Jamie, here?" He asked.

"Back there somewhere," I pointed behind me, the church was still in my view. Kenny turned looking, then made the suggestion to go back to look.

But I offered him some candy, then, "psych!"

"Oh, good one, Jamie, but seriously let's go back and look, there may be more money, come on," he carefully said.

He took some steps back, looking down at the sidewalk. I stood there digging in the candy bag and called Kenny to me, then handed him a handful of candy.

"Thanks, hum-good!" He cheerfully said.

I nodded my head yes; my mouth was filled with fire balls as we were walking the rest of the six blocks down to my house, eating all but two pieces, those I saved for Suzie.

"Later, Jamie, see you tomorrow at school, four more days to go. Hey look your Dad's home," He explained. He was right on all accounts; I nodded, then Kenny waved. I jammed the two-Bit O Honeys into my powder blue church pants pocket.

Dad was indeed home; his black Oldsmobile car was parked at the side street of our corner house. Dad was an eighteen-wheeler long-haul tractor trailer truck driver. I went into the kitchen. Dad had been sitting in his chair closest to the kitchen door. I had greeted Dad in my usual way; with a *what's up Daddy-O* then a hug. I never really showed too much happiness, fear that something bad would come next. I didn't know what it was, just a feeling I guessed that came over me. I would shut down the good feeling and it left me in a more serious mood. Yet, in my world, it was bound to happen, so I tried to keep cool.

"Jamie kiddo, my little girl- well, I should stop calling you little girl but you'll always be mine little girl," Dad said in his cheerful deep voice. He was right, I was his little girl, and laughed.

"Not so fast, Jamie," Mom said hanging up the phone and walking over to the table sitting close to Dad where I was just about to sit. Here it comes, I thought and remained standing close by. We had formed a triangle as I waited for the boom to drop.

"Hey Jamie, I got a phone call from the Father. Gus, why don't you tell Jamie what we found out and what you're going to do about it!" Mom said in a matter-a-fact- tone- of- voice. I was a little nervous, I had just taken that quarter. Nah, it couldn't have been that I thought- could it?

"Hey kiddo, it looked like you've seen a ghost. It seems like the Farther has extra camp openings at a discount price. You and your brother can go for two weeks, separate sessions, one for the girls then one for the boys." Dad said.

"Camp, I heard of that", I had said after I breathed out a heavy sigh through my puckered lips trying to keep it cool. "Cool" I had replied then thanked my parents.

I guessed that's what it meant about God working in mysterious ways; that day was filled with surprises. I was grateful and thanked God too. I had asked him for forgiveness for taking the quarter and was looking forward to camp.

What an eye-opening experience camp was for me. The country was beautiful; two weeks in West Virginia, fresh air, tent living, swimming, and away from James. Then would be his turn at camp. It all seemed liked it would change me for the better, or at least I thought. I was a pretty good kid but could swear like a sailor then. We all could in my neighborhood. I used the phrase *psych* a lot then too. Yet, I was so different from those kids. They were all *girly* girls and I was a *tomboy*. I knew I was different from some of the kids in my neighborhood, but I could blend in there. But those kids were weird, I thought. Nevertheless, I would soon learn the difference. They seemed nice most of the time. They had gasped when they heard me drop the F- bomb for the first time during the meet-and-greet in the beautiful main lodge. We all had name tags on. Four of the girls walked away as soon as the word hit their ears.

"What, did you say? I can't believe you said that, you talked like that Jamie," Kristin smilingly said as she wrinkled up her cute nose in disgust.

"Yeah, you're just plain rude! My parents told me there would be kids from Pittsburgh at our camp this year and here you are! Come on Kristin let's get away from her!" Nancy said frowning, then turning away.

I replied with a "yeah, Nancy, get the hell away from me- psych!"

"No, Nancy, stay here, you don't have to leave just because she told you to. I think she's kind of cool in a rude way! I meant you're different, and what's up with this psych stuff?" Kristin inquired.

I didn't care if they had name tags on, I didn't want to know their names and had planned on staying to myself as much as possible. There was an awkward silence, then Kristin had smiled, then I did.

I had watched the T.V. called life from my world, sizing people up checking out where they were coming from, a good place or bad and this was no different. Weird or not, I could tell Kristin was cool in a country kind of way. It just seemed as if the three of us out of five campers needed to relax, to enjoy one another's company. And in between swimming (my favorite), campfires, camp songs being sung, hikes, fishing, positive team work and three delicious meal at the main lodge we did just that. I had taught Kristin and Nancy some things. Like how to be cool- city cool, how to cuss and use the word *psych* in everyday conversation as we would walk each morning back from breakfast to the camp grounds.

"Yeah, Jamie, I think Nancy's pretty cool, *not*, wait I meant to said psych", Kristin said, then she laughed so hard she almost fell down the side of the hill. I tried to catch her, but couldn't reach her. Kristin grabbed onto my right shoulder with her right hand. I planted my feet firmly into the ground and braced myself. Then she hopped on her left foot regaining her balance. If it wasn't for her quick-wittedness and the use of her straight athletic body, she would have fell down the hill.

"That, was a close one I thought," Kristin said.

But she had told me it was nothing, her parents made her take ballet and she hated it.

"Very funny, ass, are you okay Kristin? Jamie did all the work "psych!" But you were so graceful. I wanted to applaud you, "psych." I could have probably done the same thing "psych", I have theses short legs," Nancy playfully said flicking her long blonde hair back from her slightly chunky pretty face as if the wind seemed to comb through her hair. Kristin looked at me, I looked at her then we both looked at Nancy.

We yelled "you got it!"

Then I said "high five, Nancy"; that was something else we had to work on, but it was cool, we had a week of camp to go.

"All, kidding aside, Jamie, you're cool, you're like a big sister or something - you really care I saw the concern in your face!" Kristin said.

I thanked her, then informed them both that if word got out that I was nice I would kick their asses; "psych" then laughter filled the tent.

However, they had taught me so much more. It wasn't the vocabulary definition of the word dysfunctional, or how Mom would say your cross to bear, but the meaning of it was revealed in their actions because the "dysfunctional" simply wasn't there. Instead, a sense of a good life was noted in their everyday life. I saw that it was not in my everyday life. I learned that Nancy and Kristin "The Tommy-Hawks" (I made up the name), and the rest of the campers: "The Eagles", "The Bears", "The Scouts" and "The Birds", all knew what a kid's life was supposed to be like. I liked the birds name because it had represented the different types of girls in their camp, so they said. But all knew what a kid's life was supposed to be like; minus one- me! It was in their everyday life conversations, the way that they carried themselves, in the stories of their family's life's and how they lived; my mind was blown! Those kids were truly weird and different, and I wanted to be a kid like them too.

However, we had some things in common, we were the Tommy - Hawks

who needed to not be so anxious at times for our own various reasons, who loved being silly and having fun. We enjoyed the beauty of the starlit sky, and sat around the crackling camp fire, sang songs and ate s'mores. I loved the times we sat quietly and simply listened to the sounds and breath in all that nature had to offer, it seemed to calm me. Yet, the biggest thing we had in common happen right before we went to bed, we said the Lord's Prayer, and that was something to hold on to after finding out about my life.

But there was that one night, the night before the last night. I remembered it well, I had a whole day to ponder over it. I was miserable, and on top of it all, I felt all that I was not. Until, I heard the camp counselor make the announcement that there would be a night swim, I did mention I liked to swim. It was all I could think of as I was scarfing down my dinner. I ran the half mile from the Eagle Hawk main lodge back to the Tommy- Hawk grounds where the Tommy-Hawk flag we made flew high and got my swim gear and flashlight ready for the night.

The pool was a beauty, an 8-foot, fenced-in, one. I sat on the grass outside the fence with my gear rolled in my towel that I had laid beside me. I was putting my hair in a high ponytail; while I watched the counselors string the white lights and placed tiki torches in each of the four corners. The tail end of my ponytail almost touched the back of my neck and my auburn color was turning light by the sun. There was a baseball game going on in the field behind me but I didn't care. I had imagined the night swim was a special event for me and I was waiting for my guests to arrive; it was better than thinking about the last night. I enjoyed watching the lights being strung so much that I'd asked if I could help, and I did.

We strung the lights alongside the fence and above it, it was great. It was a perfect night for a swim. I sat there poolside looking in awe of it all. It was gorgeous, how the strung white lights seemed to have mixed into the starlit sky. I recalled I had sat for quite a while before I swam, I felt so small- humble. Then I heard the sounds of campers that drew me away; the splashing of water and smell of the pool water mixed with the crisp night air. I breathe it in then made my way to the diving board. A back dive into the water that welcomed me into its warmth. I swam underwater until the 5 ft. mark then continued wading in the water to the shallow end of the pool. We had enjoyed two hours of swimming fun.

We walked back to the Tommy-Hawk flag, flashlights in hand with beams of lights moving in all directions; wearing our bathing suits and flip flops, towels of various colors and lengths strung over shoulders, some were wrapped around camper's waist. Some wore two-piece suits like Nancy and Kristin with a floral pattern, and others had the one-piece swim suits. Mine was a black one-piece Speedo suit. I picked it to help slim down my broader shoulders and busty breasts; yet, it complemented my waist line and narrow hips. The different campers spread out to go in their various directions to their camp grounds and said their goodbyes. We kept walking east and we hung back from the rest of the Tommy-Hawks stopping at times to horse around. I placed my flashlight up to my chin, we all did, in attempting to made scary faces and creepy sounds. The sounds were great but Nancy's face was too pretty of a baby-face and Kristin with her sculpted face could look a little scary but she had a silly grin on her face. I on the other hand, rolled my big dark brown eyes in the back of my head until the white showed then showed my teeth like a snarling wolf and growled! I knew somethings about frightening faces but maybe I went too far. It really freaked Nancy out to the point that she almost cried.

"Stop, you're really scaring me, no freaky psych about it," Nancy stammered, then scared which drew the counselor's attention and we received a sharp reprimand to settle down! So, we then had a group hug, it seemed to work, but that was quite awkward for me, but it was done.

We reached the Tommy- Hawk camp grounds but Nancy didn't want to go into the tent right away.

Kristin managed to calm her down by talking about the beauty of the night and how it went on-and-on into space reaching heaven. And before I knew it, we were holding hands, flashlights off, heads tilted back gazing in wonderment, or perhaps in awe at the awesomeness of the night, then began to pray.

◊

I had one of those old nightmares the night before my last night at camp. I was thankful for the night swim; it made my last night memory of camp a good one. We had packed our belongings pretty much all that day, besides having meals, sweeping out the tents, picking up any trash that was on the grounds and having a scavenger hunt of the lost and found items- it was a clever way to clean up the camp. Those dreams always ended in me waking to a wet bed. I thought those days were behind me. I haven't had any in four years but there I was. I had woken in a terrible fright, my horrendous screams woke Kristin and she shined her flashlight from across the tent on me. Nancy woke up, yet she was half asleep; she was a heavy sleeper. I was soaking wet when Kristin came over to my cot, flashlight in hand. She kept the light low to the floor then sat down at the foot of my cot, then instantly jumped up! I was so embarrassed but Kristin was cool.

"It's okay Jamie, it's okay, it was only a bad dream. Go back to bed Nancy everything's okay, Jamie just had a bad dream, right Jamie?" Kristin asked.

I replied with a "right" and sat up.

Kristin then stood at the foot of her cot from mine and we waited in silence for a moment, which felt like forever to me, making sure Nancy wasn't awake in the top bunk.

Kristin sprang into action rifling through her trunk pulling out a pink fitted sheet.

"Here, get up and take that wet sheet off, flip the mattress over and we'll put this one on," she said. I did what she said then changed my clothes, placing the pissy things in a plastic bag and fresh air returned to the tent.

"I'm not so cool, huh, Kristin?"

"Yeah you are, I wet myself once too. Mom had said my pediatrician said it was because I was stressed out because Daddy didn't get my horse then. It didn't happen again since I got my JoJo," Kristin said.

I smile a quick smile and told her okay.

"It's cool Jamie, it's our little secret and if you tell anyone I was nice to you I'll kick your ass "psych!" she jokily demanded. Then we laughed, had a quick hug, then Kristin returned to her cot; it was lights out. I could tell from the start that Kristin was cool. Yet, I had cried myself back to sleep that night.

I was confused, felt anxious, was irritated, but most of all felt betrayed, but I was home. I had a bittersweet sense about me while walking the house room after room. I saw images of past sorrows and pain whether I wanted to view them or not. So, many horrors, I thought the images consumed my mind and covered what appeared to be every room of the entire house; as fleeting moments of happiness went by too. Oh, there were far too few, I was certain there had to be more. The house looked old- worn but clean- the windows were opened but the air that came in wasn't as fragrant as the county air and the house felt empty to me, void of love, love whatever that was. But at least, James wasn't there, I thought.

Those kids at camp had their perfect little lives – "Oh, I was so stress out over a horse"- a horse! They were brought up so well-adjusted, led meaningful lives and had worthwhile dreams. What did I have? My life was a lie; kids weren't supposed to live like I did! I, on-the-other-hand was flawed, wounded, broken, undermined and perhaps sick! What a life I had. Was it a mere flip of a coin? No, I thought, it had to be more; right God? I had thrown both of my arms up high in the air and looked up to the ceiling. I had to get out of that house. So, I got my boy's lime green ten speed bike out from the basement so I could cruise.

And I cruised, to get away from it all, to get away from me. Thank God it was a warm sunny dry day and I had a much-needed break from James. I had noted the air wasn't as clean smelling as the county air as I pedaled my bike fast down the side street by my house to pick up speed. I stopped pedaling and let my bike coast at a fast speed. Then I raised my arms parallel in line with my shoulders and created a wingspan, tilting my head back as far as it could go, closed my eyes and I would glide. I felt free in those moments, fleeting as they were, nevertheless free. I was never looking to find me; I looking for what God wanted me to be - what love was all about. I had refused to believe that this state of life was it. Then I heard Timmy and Kenny as they rode by on their bikes.

"Look who's back, wake up sleeping beauty," Timmy whispered in a sarcastic annoying tone. I opened one eye, then the other. I was pissed turning my bike around riding back up the street with Kenny by my right and Timmy rode his dark green ten-speed bike off to the side of Kenny and slightly behind.

"She's wasn't asleep, she was a beautiful bird, "psych." Come on Jamie, snap out of it, it's bakery shopping day," Kenny said, his voice had made its change- it sounded good and I told him so. I had forgotten what day it was; Kenny was always prepared. He had three shopping bags that hung from his blue bike's handle bars. And no matter how hot it was on bakery day he would wear his lucky faded tie-dye T-shirt and blue jean just in case he fell off his bike. I thought wearing that t- shirt was funny.

"Yeah, Jamie, turn that boy's bike of yours around and let's go. She doesn't look like a boy anymore," Timmy reminded.

I told him to just follow his nose; he could smell the wonderful scent of fresh bakery goods that was there for the taking. I knew the way there and we were on our way. Timmy was quite the looker with his green eyes, slightly freckled face.

I used my busty rack by pushing my shoulders back then sat on my bike seat, used my wit, and sometimes charm to distract the male bakery workers while they were on their lunch break in front of the bakery. Some stood while others were sitting on wooden folding chair. While Kenny and Timmy went around the back to the opened garage where the freshly baked donuts and breads were on cooling racks. The workers were used to our routine, but it was different that day. Those guys were like sharks, cat-calling, and the things one guy said was just plan rude. I'd learned that from Nancy from camp- just plan rude!

"Hey girly, my name is Pete I know your friends are back at the racks stealing, I don't care. Yinz can have a whole rack before the truck comes if you want." Pete said.

I just looked at him from across the street as he got up from his chair walking over to the side walk curb. I placed my left foot on the bike pedal then whistled. It was the one whistle for a ten count to "clear out of there" code. Two whistles meant get out.

"Hey, it's okay, you and me could work something out. What's your name, come here, I don't bite unless you went me too," Pete boastfully said as he was walking across the street with a swagger in his walk as if he was some type of tough guy in his all white bakery uniform. He was brushing back his slicked-back black hair and flexing his arm muscles. I rode away whistling twice.

"Hey, bastard you can't talk to her like that!" Timmy yelled as he rounded the corner at a fast speed then threw a donut then picked up some rocks and threw them at Pete too!

"Let's go Timmy, let's go Jamie," Kenny said, we were at the top of the street by then when we heard yelling.

"Yeah, go Jamie, I'll see you late babe." Pete instructed and he laughed. I pedaled faster, we all did then till we were about a block away from Timmy's house, about ten city blocks away from the bakery, and stopped there.

I got off my bike, parking it on the street by the curb as if it was a car; the guys followed suit, and then we all sat on the curb.

"Nice going Kenny, you said our names," Timmy yelled in his usual tough voice when he thought he had to address or confront someone about something. I watched the two of them as they bickered back and forth like a tennis match.

"I, just got nervous, I didn't know what was going on Timmy, Jamie – I'm an ass I messed up I'm sorry," Kenny said.

I waved my hand in the air at Kenny shrugging him off then said, "whatever!"

He really didn't care; he was too busy dividing up the day's take into the three bags. Then I informed the guys that I was out. I had enough, I'd did all the bakery shopping I had needed to do. Besides, it wasn't right; it was kind of fun when we were younger kids.

"No, don't do that we just need to lay low for a while. Here Jamie take your bag," Kenny ordered.

I got up and walked to my bike. Timmy got up and took my bag from Kenny which was filled with mostly donuts, then stepped down off the curb. He was attempting to hand me the bag. I told him to keep it, I didn't want it, and I thought, if he only knew.

"You, cool Jamie?" Timmy asked softly. I told him yeah but I could tell that he wasn't quite convinced that I was alright. I told the guys I had to go, I had chores that needed done at home. Then thanked Timmy for coming to my rescue. Hopping on my bike then rode around the corner headed up the street to my house which was only a few blocks away.

1977

Time had gone by; it was a Friday after school, a chilly sunny March day in 1977. The weather was much better than the coldest month on record for Pittsburgh in January, its frigid temperatures 13 below and gusting winds. Nevertheless, sometime had passed since, I rode my bike around that corner in late July and returned to my same old everyday life. I had learned some things during my time at camp, but how to put it all together was another, and to attempt to fix things was a whole other matter with problems of its own. I had enough on my plate. I had decided I would leave the how I would leave that mess of my so-called life up to God to workout. My imaginary and obscured world made no sense to me for the most part. Other than, I didn't give up on hope, yet sometimes I thought hope gave up on me! What did I know, I was fourteen going on some type of adult age? Timmy and Kenny had moved away, how I missed the guys. And I didn't interact much with the other neighborhood kids anymore.

I had got home from school when I was just about to start on a sink full of dishes when I found myself looking instead out the kitchen window. I saw about six kids I knew who were hanging out across the street and watched them as they were horsing around. I opened the window carefully not to distract and only slightly so I could hear them better. I had imagined that I was there with them too. And just about the time I was going to smile, Ryan noticed me watching.

"What the hell, you looking at Jamie!" Ryan asked.

"Go clean your house!" He ordered.

I gave him the finger.

"Leave her alone Ryan, she's not bothering you," Lori demanded then pushed Ryan in the chest.

"She gave me the finger, what about that Lori?" Ryan asked.

"Only after you started with her Ryan!" She corrected.

"Hi Jamie!" Lori said.

I waved and Lori waved back. They all stared at me then I closed the window with its squeaks. I turned away nervously staring down at the piled high dishes in the sink. I could still hear them, they were laughing. I glanced to the right and noticed I didn't close the damn window all the way, but it didn't matter the sounds of the laughed soon faded away. Afterwards my imagination kicked in I focused on the group of kids; I focused on Lori and then I thought.

There they are teenagers in their teenage stages of various ages, if I had the knowledge of being a kid that you possess, who would I be, I wondered? Oh, I've struggled to be like you Lori. We are kids; a special gift from God, if I only could be a kid like you. Yet, I knew I had endured more. Yeah, Lori had her teenage fears, anxiety, and the stress that came with being a teenager; the mood swings, being a know-it-all and a pain in the ass...I was all that too. Lori complained, I heard it all at school; how she thought her world fell apart over some trivial matter at school that caused her sorrow. I laughed! I found it funny, but I shouldn't have, it was a big deal to her. However, nothing she or the others, for that matter, described in their everyday lives were like the impact of my troubles, that was for sure, and I had no one to talk to about it! And this was in my own neighborhood. I was at the bottom of the barrel it seemed. Yet, I persevered, I coped; used my wits and prayed for a better tomorrow, tomorrow, a better tomorrow!

I struggled in school too. Heck, I remembered that one day, it was a Tuesday morning after a "good time" was had at my expense by the donut-man, off to Elementary School I went. I recalled thinking it was a good thing that my desk was in the back of the classroom due to alphabetical order seating. It was good for me most of the time, but not that day. It would soon be my turn to go to the front of my first-grade class to read. While I remained in a frightened, bewilder insecure state, it was my turn to read, the teacher had started calling the kids up to read from the back of the classroom, lucky me.

I was walking up to the front of the classroom by ways of using the center aisle passing the five rows of kids seated at their desks to my left and to my right. I had noticed some of the kids made faces; placing their hands over their noses. My feet felt like lead and my heart beat heavy in what seemed to be in my throat. I swallowed hard, but my saliva had all since gone and it felt so dirty. The teacher handed me the opened book.

"Here Jamie, take this you forgot your book. Quiet down class! Jamie's going to read page three. And I want you all to follow along. Anytime you're ready Jamie," she said as she scowled down at me through her glasses that sat low on her nose. I tried to read but the words didn't come out right. And they laughed, laughter filled the classroom, twenty, no nineteen kids and one teacher laughing and laughed at my expense. I had wished that I could laugh too but not even that came out. I had thought it would have been better for me if I only could have laughed along too or even better, if I could explain, but I knew it would only make it worse.

"Okay, that's quite enough boys and girls; be quiet, fun time is over. Jamie go back to your seat!" She ordered.

I walked back watching every step I took my legs felt so wobbly but I kept watch not to look up and hummed a tune in my head not to hear their words, but I did, but I didn't cry, then!

There were no tears during lunch either, but oh, it was so hard to eat. I barely ate for all their teasing and taunting and I was so hungry because I didn't have time to eat at home. Before the lunch period was over everyone in the cafeteria knew that I was that stinky girl that couldn't read. But I didn't cry then either, I simple bit on the scar tissue on the inside of the bottom and sides of my mouth.

I had managed to get to the bathroom during recess and was able to clean up a bit. I saw my morning teacher in the hallway as I came out of the bathroom and she handed me a note to take home, then told me I smelled much better. I had told her thanks and kept my head down as I was walking toward the classroom to return to class when the end of recess bell had rung. I felt somewhat better and tucked the note in my blue jeans left pocket. I knew that the afternoon teacher was strict- a stickler for the rules regarding kids' behavior in her classroom - so I began to feel even better.

My school was around the corner from the front of my church and was five blocks down the street on the next corner on, but on the right side of the street corner from the church. I believed it was about twelve blocks for me to walk from school to home. And I would have to walk it alone, James had an after-school club that day. Then it happens, the bell rung ending the school day, I just had to make it home. I tried taking my time lingering in the halls, stopping to tie my tennis shoes, drank from the water fountain in hope that my classmates would get tired of waiting for me and leave. One of the kids from my class ran ahead of me opened the door leaning on it with her body and held it opened for me.

Exposing me to the kids that were there waiting for me just outside the door. I took a deep breath in then and let it out slowly, then went outside. I was kicked, my hair was pulled and reminded how stupid I was and was told to go home and wash my clothes. It was a long walk home, I couldn't run because I was surrounded, but they scattered like rats when my neighbor honked his car horn as he drove by. I didn't cry then but I ran into the safety of my fenced-in yard, about a block away. I knew I would feel better once I got into the house, Thank God I thought for Mr. S.

I burst through the door sobbing which ended quickly, Mom was there.

"What, the hell's wrong with you Jamie?" Mom asked "You let them damn kids beat you up again, didn't you?"

"Go in your room, get a sock, then get my piggy bank out of my room and bring them both to me," She commanded.

I did what I was told to do returning with a pair of socks and Mom's pink piggy bank filled with nickels. I was so frightened, I thought I would have been able to go straight to my room to cry. Mom placed nickels into one of the white socks then made a knot in the top of the sock and handed it to me closing my fingers over the sock which made a fist. But I was left-handed, I guessed she just forgot.

"Here, first thing tomorrow morning when you're in the school courtyard, Jamie, I want you to sock the hell out of the first kid you see that beat you up! Make sure you're in the courtyard so the other kids can see. Beat that kid up and any other kid you see that did it to you!" Mom demanded. "And if you don't, Jamie, when you get home, I'll beat you!"

A look of terror came over my face, not for what Mom had told me I had to do, but that look I knew, that look that meant terror for me! Let's just say the nickel sock was in my left hand the next day and I was not teased or beat up any more.

◊

I had just about finished with the pile of dishes when Suzie walked into the kitchen, it was later in the evening close to dinner time, but I could go off for some time in my own little world.

"You're still doing dishes?" Suzie asked. "Here's some more; what's with the silly looking grin on your face, stop it!"

She replied, "Oh wait, it's Friday that means fishing for cash tomorrow, yeah!"

I'd dropped my silly grin and had smirked behind her back, as she was walking to her chair, then sat down. I loved to smirk and was still doing so while I started warshing the dish; cup and spoon she gave me I was clicking and clunking the spoon to the cup intentionally to annoy her while she sat there doing a crossword puzzle that was in the Pittsburgh Press Newspaper. She looked up at times and had gave me a couple of dirty looks. I could see her from my peripheral vision, yet the noise that I had made wasn't a good enough distraction So, I stopped and informed her that I was done. Then I had made three steps to my left to leave the kitchen but Suzie had cleared her voice, I looked as she was motioning me to sit down; what now I had thought.

"Tell, me really Jamie, what do you do for that money?" Suzie inquired

I had explained it to Suzie several time before but I guessed she didn't care to listen. One more time would put her mind at easy yet I clearly understood why I didn't bother anymore to explain myself. "You lie, Jamie who do you get the money from?" She demanded of me. I had suggested she should come along with me and that I would be leaving at 7:35 a.m. in the morning. That way she could see for herself and it would put her mind at easy. She mocked me then, sarcastically told me that I could leave the kitchen and did I, gladly.

Off to my retreat I went, the attic, I felt welcomed there in my room. No one ever came up there anymore. I laid on my twin bed. It was the first time I'd kicked back to relax since I came home from school that day. There was not much to my bed room but I didn't care. I had an old table and a lamp, things that Mom gave Jennifer and she left them in the room because she had graduated to Raymond's old room, lucky her. And I had won a 12' black and white T.V. set from the grand reopening of Giant Eagle, that was cool, and of course my prize possession; my radio. The excitement was building as I laid there jamming to some tunes for Saturday morning to arrive. Let me tell you, Friday nights were known as trucker night at Jack's bar, his wife made a great fish sammitch (sandwich) and Dad would buy some at times. At closing time most of the truckers staggered across the street to the dirt and gravel dimly lit parking lot to their cabs section of their trucks to sleep it off. Most of the trucks would be gone by 7:35 a.m. in the morning but I would check by looking out my window using Raymond's binoculars before I left for those one or two stragglers. And when they left, that's when I sprang into action, leaving the house. Jumping on my bike flash light in hand but I wouldn't need it for long because the sun would rise soon. Just about the time it took me to ride the two and a half blocks to the lot it would be light enough to see without the use of my light. But I had a great head light for the bike ride down and I quite enjoyed the chilly breeze, it reminded me that I was alive. Off the bike, it was better to be on foot while fishing for cash. Fishing for cash, Friday fish sammitch-fishing, you get the picture and I was reeling in the dough! I could pick up anywhere between twenty to thirty-five dollars on a good morning. I picked up coins, ones, five- and ten-dollars bills, and sometime the occasional twenty- dollar bill, but mostly ones. I had a good amount stashed away too. I was able to buy my bike the one year, which was the high light of that year. I felt sorry sometimes for the truckers, they needed the money too just like my Dad needed his. Good morning it was in deed, thirty-three dollars take, not bad. I even gave Suzie fifteen dollars. You may be thinking that was nice of me, what a good kid; but no, I did it because I knew Suzie, she was by far not done with the where I got the money line of question. So, I gave her something to think about; I was being a brat, yet in a good way I thought. I would save the rest to help out here and there and maybe two dollars for the collection plate at church. I thought fishing for cash meant food for the family and then fishing to collect people. Yet, I often wondered when I would be caught, maybe I wasn't good enough, so I was told - whatever!

The week that followed spelled disaster for Jack; his wife of thirty-seven years literally dropped dead of a heart attack in the bar's kitchen during lunch prep. Jack was devastated and closed the bar the next day for good. But Jack liked our family, we did eat a lot of fish sammitches (sandwiches) between Dad buying them when he wasn't on the road and everyone pitching in. I would even hit my stash from time to time, but not often because I needed to keep it quiet. I didn't want to put too much attention on the fact that I had money or it would have been taken from me. We got two, that was all we needed was two, two could feed eight because of the two big pieces of haddock fish would be cut in half then placed on Town talk bread.

I was always in and out of the bar picking up our food orders. Then I got a job sweeping the bar floor at 10 o' clock before Jack opened for the day. We were like family, but I thought only two dollar a day was a little light. I was treated nicely and if there was any left-over-fish I could have some, but no bun. That was fine with me, I wasn't a big bread eater. Except when I had peanut butter and grape jelly and fried jumbo sammitches, then I'd eat it. Just smelling it made my mouth water, sometimes some things were not meant to be shared. Jack was a good man and his wife too who mainly kept to her work smiling at me on the occasion. She would come out to the bar to put out the hard-boiled eggs and sometimes tell me that it was time for me to go home. She didn't believe that women had no place in or at the bar. I was just a girl that should have been home doing chores, if she only knew. Jack had given the family most of the food that was in the bar's kitchen refrigerator, but not the batter. I watched Jack as he had dump it down the kitchen sink drain. He had said the secret to the great taste of the fish was in the batter and that it would be going to the grave with Ruth! Ruth, I thought what a pretty name, I never knew it. It was sad she passed away; she was in her eighty's when she left. I had said a prayer, lit a candle in her memory and had put an extra dollar in the plate in Ruth's honor. No more great fish sammitch and no more fishing for cash for me, and Jack moved away the following week. We didn't even know exactly when he left, he was simply just gone. I had wished I knew he was just going to leave so quickly: I would have given him a hug that day he gave us the food; he was my family.

But sorrow wasn't quite done, relentless as it was. I liked to call it sorrow's woes because sorrow was sometimes so plentiful in a given time span that it had its own woes- Ha-ha! It was good to laugh, laughed at myself at times, it helped to ease the pain. Suzie's sorrow's woes were a part of me, draped on my shoulders like a cape. I took it on. I assumed the extra burden, it was a part of the caregiver role, and coupled with my turbulent teenage years I was a mess. However, I managed to put my best foot forward (pardon the cliché) but I was good under pressure in times of crisis. I had pushed my sorrow's woes pretty far down years ago, but I had to admit at times, I had to swallow hard to contain my emotions. I had attempted to keep my venting and/or pity parties to a minimum. Yet did it really matter? I was the only one that heard me; well God too but I sometimes thought it may have been cold in heaven at times and he had his ear muffs on- Ha-Ha! Thank God for music, my imagination, dance, prayer and alcohol. In no particular order, they helped alleviate the effects of the affects of my life. And I had grown fond of three: the music-I could get lost in it, my imagination- it amused me and pray- I prayed for guidance, for a better day. It could be a source of comfort, and I prayed for others, but always Suzie.

Suzie suffered a devastated blow too. It was a high point to her sorrow's tragic events in her life, but this one was the biggest! Suzie's first-born son died a horrendous death, only after he suffered a great deal of pain before he left this world. Her son Raymond was a special treat to her; she placed him on a pedestal and in her forever he would remain there. Raymond could walk in a room and became the subject- all would place their focus on him. He was 6ft., tall, muscular built but not too much, with an olive complexion; his Mom's second favorite color. And he was intelligent, things just came to him with little effort, and he was a Marine veteran.

His wife was expecting their first child in a month's time, a little someone Raymond couldn't wait to meet. I loved Raymond. He paid attention to me, showed me concern, and he was cool. I enjoyed our time together and often felt so alone and sad when he would leave.

"Okay Jamie, you're done with your chores, it's our time together," Raymond cheered.

"Let's do this," I had replied then we jagged around slap boxing which was funny to see, I was only 5' 4 ft. We slap boxed to the fridge where I then turned to open the fridge up and I got the jumbo out. We loved that smell of the jumbo frying. I watched from the side of the stove while Raymond fried it up. We ended up bobbing our heads to the beat we heard from the popping of the jumbo in the pan. Then I would dance around the kitchen while Raymond sung acapella using that great bass voice of his. It was classic. He was great at singing Doo-Wop and Motown, and was in a band. But he preferred singing back up and playing his bass guitar. Then we made and ate our fried jumbo sammitches (sandwiches). Raymond had worshed the pan and our lunch dishes, sometimes splashing water at me. It was a special treat for me, but I had to do something so I wiped the kitchen table off then worshed my hands. It had become our normal routine, still it was strange to me seeing Raymond at the sink, worshing the dishes because that was my job. But after sometime had passed, I was cool with it and I would playfully harass him about getting those dishes done.

"Okay, boss the dishes are done, time for your drawing lesson, Jamie," Raymond sang as he placed his art kit on the kitchen table. Raymond was an artist in his own right; chalk portraits was his forte. He taught me how to draw profiles of men and women's faces, eyes, lips and how to accent the cheekbones with shading. I was okay at it, but I didn't have a talent for it. He was quite fond of the cheekbone area of the face; I had often wondered if it was because he had high cheekbones, but I never asked. I loved watching him bring a blank sheet of art paper to life. Creating a collage of various faces of beautiful people right before my eyes. Ah, the wonderment of it all, and I wondered what it was like to be him.
"Pretty good Jamie," "psych", he chuckled, "No, you're getting it!"
"So. Jamie, seriously, you're a good listener, a caring person, patient and relentless, some good skills you need for when you get older; education too. Time to start thinking about what you're going to do with your life," he said as he put the last piece of chalk and zipped the case closed. Then we looked at one another intently, hugged and kissed, I didn't want him to leave. Raymond made a trip to the local Mary Jane neighborhood store that night that placed him in the wrong place at the wrong time; and he was shot in the chest and died later, about ten that night. I was there in the emergency room, there with Suzie. We watched as Raymond struggled for life! Suzie was by her son's side- me from my corner view. Raymond declared," What a miserable life I had!

Suzie was attempting to convince Raymond otherwise by recalling events in Raymond's life. But he died! Suzie threw up- it seemed like there was puke everywhere. At the very least it was all down Suzie's blue dress and on what was the off- white emergency room floor. She was grief stricken- Raymond her joy had died! Suzie was in need of medical attention; her vitals were taken and she was given a little oxygen and then a little white pill to calm her nerves. I had often wondered what a person with a broken spirit looked like so I could compare it to mine; I wondered no more as I looked at Suzie.

I was shocked when I heard Raymond's last words, I had thought that Raymond's life was a good one, far as my eyes could see. I was devastated, I tell you. I didn't swallow my feelings that night – no, I wept bitterly, the memory etched in my mind. Yet, Raymond sometimes used the phrase, "The struggles I have seen" and his letters he wrote to Suzie when he was in active duty always ended in him closing with, "Yours in the struggle of life." I didn't know what his struggles were, but it meant something. Raymond had his sorrow's woes too, as we all do. I wasn't the only one that held them in. We never really know what's going on in a person's life, concealed struggle! It was best if we behave lovingly to one another and were great listeners, I thought. It was truly sad how Raymond was a kind man and appeared to be happy but what laid within him we would nerve know. I hoped before I died, I could serve a purpose- not die in vain.

Ten days later, Raymond's widow had shot herself in the chest- inches away from her heart. Raymond's son was born pre-mature that afternoon and both Mother and child were doing well; Raymond had an effect on people. Yes, for seventeen months of darkness fell upon Suzie, remaining a shell of her former self. Trapped there in her bed room seemingly almost child-like at times. There within the smells of her brokenness I would cater to her every need, yet her needs in her mind were very few. Attempting to entice her to eat, bathe, to allow the shutters to be opened, the drapes to be drawn and the windows to be opened to let in life. God had worked in mysterious ways; the best way for Suzie. In that following month Suzie's eighteen months of deep grieving was lifted, Raymond's widow would drop off Suzie's grandson, and his

Mother, we never saw her again. I stood by Suzie's side, helping her raise him while his grandpa took on a second job. Suzie gave all that she was and had to the little one, not much was left for me. I knew I didn't have much of a relationship with Suzie and I missed her from time to time, but I missed Raymond the most.

1983

It was February 23, 1983, six years had gone by since Raymond left, his words still echoed in my mind. I hungered for more then what life had gave me, more then what it attempted to assign me to and what I had gave myself was not enough. I was twenty years old and wanted to help others beyond my focus of my family. I knew if I wanted to do that, I had to help myself first. To be equipped to service, college would have to wait, I needed God. So, I took a detour from the obscured aspects of my everyday life.

Mom had all her kids baptized as babies but me. I had asked her why?

"I was tired then, Jamie, and thought I would leave it up to you," Mom claimed. She paused for a moment looking as if she was thinking of something. She moved her eyes side-to-side and twisted her lip in an inquisitive manner. What was it already, I thought – out with it!

"What would you think about James being your Godfather, sponsoring you?" She asked.

Uh, I wasn't sure how to reply to that. I thought Mom's suggestion was not a good idea, nevertheless, I agreed.

"I thought it could help the two of you build a better relationship," she replied.

Okay, James and my big sister Anna it would be. I thought my suffering in silence as a child was bad, and still no voice for my inner child. But Mom placing James on me this way was like an extra burden, how could she! James be supportive to my spiritual growth? In an indirect way, I suppose. No matter, God was able and I gave the matter not another thought.

There I stood in the Episcopal Church with only Anna. I was embarrassed, red-faced and felt for a moment rejected in the house of the Lord. But then I knew better, this was James, not showing up and maybe for a good reason... breathe, Jamie just breathe, I thought. And I took two big breaths. Anna took my right hand squeezing it while she looked me in the eyes as if to say all is well. And deep inside of me I knew it was. There was a special glow from the candles that caught my eyes that accentuated the neighboring stained-glass windows, marble and organ as I took in the beauty. I felt privileged to be in the house of God.

A friend of the family, Fred, a Catholic spiritual person stood up, then proceeded to walk down the aisle, then spoke to the Vicar.

"Hi, Father, my name is Fred. I'm a Catholic, Father, can I be Jamie's Godfather?" Fred asked.

"Do you believe in Jesus Christ, Fred?" the Vicar asked.

"I do believe in our Lord and Savior Jesus Christ," He answered.

The Vicar gave Fred a pat on his arm.

"You're in, stand here Fred," He said, then guided Fred to the spot by his shoulder. I was smiling at Fred, he smiled back at me and I nodded my head in agreement. I felt relieved, a bit nervous, and extremely delighted. I knew then that I made a choice and I chose the most important decision in my life. And in my everyday life I would need to stay in prayer. I would need to maintain my relationship with God, remaining in his love, and needing to hold fast to hope. So, I repented, renounced the devil; confirming my belief in God and entered into a committed relationship- received the Holy Spirit and I was baptized. Hallelujah! Hence, stay- maintain and hold. And I would and could with God's help. I accepted an embrace from Fred then thanked him for his act of kindness toward me.

"You're welcome, Jamie, it was my pleasure and my responsibility God daughter," Fred assured. I turned and hugged Anna, then turned back to Fred. And after Anna and Fred hugged, I looked into his sincere blue-green hazel eyes and had seen an example of a believer looking back at me .At home, Mom had put out a delicious spread of food: Stuffed shells two kinds of meat and with cheese, salad, garlic bread and a half of a marble sheet cake that read "Congratulation Jamie." Ah, and the aroma was intoxicating everyone agreed. There was ten of us (minus James) plus Fred, the Vicar, and at least eight of my church members. And it was all displayed on Great Grandma's good dishes on the dining room table. I had no words. My smile was ear-to-ear. I couldn't remember if I had cake on my birthdays, I could recall being sung to. Besides, I thought my birthday was on the 19th of the month for a good portion of my life. I found out it was on the 20th when I needed my birth certificate when I applied for a job. This dinner was awkward for me, yet, a pleasant surprise.

I gave Mom an awkward hug, we seldom shown affection, yet I was Mom's back warmer on cold winter days. I would get into bed with Mom, then place my back on her back, it created warmth. I'd listened to the cracking sounds of the fire, enjoying its orange glow cast on the wall, and sometimes Mom would sing. Sad songs mainly, but I thought she had a lovely voice. Nevertheless, I thanked Mom for all her hard work, delicious food, cake, and for the use of Great Grandma's China set that I knew meant the world to her.

"I'm proud of you, Jamie," Mom informed, "You made a good decision for your life, you have to stay, maintain and hold, Jamie, it won't be easy," Goosebumps appeared on my arms and I felt a strange feeling come over me. Mom had often said I had to stay, maintain and hold, I had just got it, or some type of version of the meaning of it that day. We embraced one another and that time it was not so awkward. "Thanks, Fred, for being a stand-up guy. I thought James would have been there, would have been here, thank you Fred," Mom confirmed. I thanked Fred once again too. Time passed, and my new life's journey continued with the Lord. Although it was not new in the sense of me believing in the Lord. It was hard at times; the good things always are the hardest in my opinion. Past sorrow's woes kept tugging at me causing mayhem with my behavior at times. However, I was at a real job then, caregiver occupation of course, one that could be a possible career, my entry position days were over. I worked for children that were physically, mentally, sexually abused and neglected. Okay, I worked for myself too. Like a drug addiction counselor, I guessed, who was a former addict, my scars were deep. I believed I held a PHD in the abused business. I was trained on the job Ha-ha- like that was nothing new- it was like on-the-job-therapy for me. I was quite fond of the session on bias opinion how not to affect the kiddos that I served. And that was double for me, I had to be mindful to my inner child too. All sarcastic joking aside, there were times I had to laugh; I did learn a great deal then. I learned the technical terms of who and/or what I was labeled as - that was a treat, I did laugh about that. Although, somewhere far from the truth for me, others were spot on. Nonetheless, all the information seemed to lead to the same conclusion, a disastrous life with little to no chance of recovery is simply a vicious cycle. Still, in that intense six months of on-the-job training and courses thereafter, there was no mention of God's love. Something like love versus sorrow's woes, no wonder the outcome ended in hopeless vicious cycle for some; not me. Maybe, it would have been better for the two to work together. Oh, love may have been mentioned, but it was not relevant to the natural source; God... yeah, imagine that! The combination of the disciplines, mental and social factors that was taught along with Christian teaching would have been covering the whole person. Providing more options, choices, rather than just the symptoms, in my opinion. An "Aha" moment went right over my head then concerning my own healing process and spiritual growth, or did it?

It was my day off and my car Dad gave me was in the repair shop for minor repairs and routine maintenance. It wasn't due to be completed until that evening. The kitchen phone rang, the ringer was set on loud for some reason, and when it rang it startled Mom and I.

"Answer the telephone, James, you're right there!" Mom yelled, "I'll cook something in a bit."

"Yeah, okay Mom, I heard it, I'm just hungry," James replied as he closed the fridge door. Mom and I were putting the groceries away while James answered the phone on the fifth ring in his usual rude manner.

"Yeah, what do you want!" he barked at the caller followed by a line of rapid questions, then threw the light blue receiving end of the wall mounted kitchen phone at me. I apologized for James' rudeness by simply stating sorry, followed by a hello. Yet, I knew when I finished talking that I should not have told my boss that I would work the shift. James threw his head back and laughed because he knew what was coming next. I watched as he laughed at me, James was outright a good-looking young man with his sculptured facial features with those eyes of his. I searched for the proper words then attempted to speak.

"No Jamie, wish in one hand and shit in the other and see what you get," James said sarcastically. Mom gave him the look of redirection.

"Yeah, I'll take you to work Jamie," he said with a sly look on his face. I thanked him and thought maybe it was his way of making up for not being there of me when I was baptized. Mom smiled. She sat at the kitchen table chopping onions prepping for dinner when James slowly pulled the chair out from the kitchen table and sat down, I remained standing and patient.

"So, what time you have to be there," he asked.

I replied 3 o'clock, he looked at his watch.

"So, it's where Kelly lived right next to the gas station?" he inquired.

I then add to the directions, four blocks down then a right.

I had ten dollars I could give him for gas, then reached in my blue jean pocket and extended it to him.

"Yeah, I was just about to ask you about that, this will do. Hurry along and get ready to go before I change my mind," he said sarcastically and I did what he had told me to do. I was puzzled though, for one that he said yes- what was the change in his attitude towards me? Never mind Mom's look, I wondered if it had anything to do with me recently taking on a spiritual humbling interaction with him? Two, that was the longest the two of us spoke to one another without an argument and three, that I would be in his truck. And finally, we would be together for the first time going somewhere for quite some time. I must tell you, I shuttered! I was a little concerned, yet glad for the ride and figured I would trust God.

Dad always said, "You've got to be at work early it's better than being on time!"

I only hoped that James had remembered what Dad said too. I returned to the kitchen, it was a little steamy there, Mom had the big pot filled with water on the stove and it was at the boiling point. James and Mom sat and were talking about some girl he had met. Then Mom got up from her chair and threw a hand full of salt into the pot and a puff of white like a cloud rose up from the pot. I stood, waiting for a pause in their conversation then informed James in a quiet manner that I was ready to go. I didn't want him to think that I was telling him what to do. There was a quick "see you, Mom" from both James and I, then we glanced at each other, then did a double take and Mom chuckled at the sight of our reaction as we had spoken at the same time. Mom told us to be good and off we went.

The ride to work: James looked down at his watch and I at mine, it was 2:15 p.m. on the dot that hot Sunday in July. When James drove his old gray Ford pick-up truck onto the parkway East headed for exit ten at the time.

"I, have 2:15 p.m." James indicated I nodded once to inform of the same time. "I'm, going to drive slow for you to ease you into the ride!" James pointed out. He drove what he considered to be a conservative 68 mph, 13 mph over the posted speed limit at that time. The wind from the opened window messed-up my long hair. So, I pinned it back with some of Mom's bobby pins hoping for the best, and just in time. "Here we go!" He uttered turning on his new stereo cassette tape player blasting Rock-N- Roll as he hit the gas pedal, he drove 80 mph. Bobbing and weaving through light traffic like a boxer who dodged his opponent's punches. The Rock-N-Roll music was like it was the crowd that cheered him on. He sang along with the singer; it was more like screaming at the top of his voice which made me grip the panel door handle tightly and began to pray. A long stretch of highway laid ahead; the wide-open road seemed to challenge him and he answered the call. Then traveling at 95 mph that old truck of his darted up the road! I had thought I had lost a lung behind and was panting! Other vehicles looked as if they were blurs of colors reds, whites and greens. The music was booming, I barely heard the whoosh sound as we passed the others by! I felt the power of the engine and I had to admit it was invigorating for a moment in a strange way! However, that soon changed as James came up fast on another truck's bumper and had to quickly swerve to the right out of the fast land passing the red pick-up truck. I took a quick breath in and held it! Then with a quick left

James drove back into the fast line just in front of the red truck. Everything looked as if it was happening in slow motion. James then darted off, tearing up the pavement at 100 mph. It all happen so fast; I swear I could smell the road. Then I exhaled slowly through my teeth and closed my eyes for not even a second to thank God. Thank you, that the other driver didn't panic, I'm not sure he or she had seen James' gray truck moving back into the fast lane or possibly at any time.

James made a quick search of my face for, I imagined, signs of terror but none were there. If he had looked a few seconds ago the horror he would have seen. My eyes felt as if they were bulging out of my eyes sockets and sheer fright seemed to have taken my scream away. It felt as though I felt my heart beat throughout my entire body and that was a new feeling. And I could see the whites of my knuckles! Thank God too, I didn't scream and that James didn't look at me then or I'd have screamed and startled James; we would have been no more! I let out a heavy sigh attempting to slow down my rapid beating heart and kept telling myself to breathe. James' adrenaline was high but he eased up on the gas pedal as his truck began to shake. He turned down the music to listen; the engine was knocking.

"Easy, Betty – easy girl, slow down!" he told his truck.

But despite it all, I was thankful to God that things worked out as they did, of course. Besides that, I couldn't show James any fear; to show him fear then would only add to his high. I had been covered by his mighty shadow all my life. I didn't dare shine, not even in my fright, to do so would be to over shine him in his excitement, in his sense of control; that could have been dangerous for me. So no, I remained still and was happy that we didn't get killed, loosened my hand grip and closed my eyes.

"Easy Betty, cool down girl!" he told his truck.

I felt the truck slowing to what felt like a normal speed, then opened my eyes as it seemed I had opened them in sync with the motion of the right turn we had made.

Then the ride was over, the truck, James and I came to a jerking stop. James immediately looked at his watch, I slowly removed my hand from the door handle slowly opening it, it hurt so bad it was throbbing and was so white. I watched as the blood returned to it, it felt so numb. James put the truck in park and turned off the music. The truck's engine had a heavy revved up sound to it then and smelling of oil.

"Yes, 2:30 p.m.!" James Cheered.

We looked at each other for a not so awkward second, James smiled, I smiled back but mine was a closed mouth smile. I remembered thinking how nice and white his teeth were, looking at them from a different view.

"Yeah, I got you here in 15 minutes, Jamie, you have 30 minutes before work, how's that for being early!" James praised turning his body towards me.

"I'm, impressed. I tried to scare the shit out of you, that's why I told you I would take you! You didn't even scream when I came close to that red truck, that was a close one!" he proclaimed.

I told James that he was a good driver, thank God and it all worked out well; that Dad would have been proud of him getting me to work 30 minutes early. I thought not, Dad would have preferred it if you drove safe, taking away less time that I would have to myself before I had to start my shift. But I couldn't say that.

James nodded his head with an agreeable grin on his face. I had thanked him for the ride, then we smiled. The hairs on James arms stood up. After I had seen that I reached over and opened the door with my left hand and got out of the truck. I walked around the front of the truck turning my head towards the windshield of the truck and smiled at James again, then went and stood on the sidewalk at his driver side of the truck's door. I stood there in amazement, watching him as he slowly drove away. The truck still had the same sound and smell to it; I hoped for his safe trip. And just as I was about to turn away, James hit his horn – beep; then extending his left arm out of the truck's window held it there as a wave goodbye. I immediately raised my left forearm from the elbow up extending it close towards my shoulder, palm opened towards James and held it there. And I watched James as he looked through his rear-view mirror at me as he drove away from view. It was in those moment that I realized that James cared for me and I had forgiven him. That wave for me was like a hello; tears formed in my eyes, I thanked God for that journey as it was more than just a ride to work for me and I thought for James too. Then I said a prayer for James' safe return. And as time went on in my everyday life, I found myself worn-out at times, from my sorrow's woes, they tugged at me often. I took on a lot of problems, it appeared, which did not exist or were not known about when I entered my job. But I thought James and I were good. I often relied on my stay, maintain, and hold concept of my controlled spiritual walk with God and it had been reduced to remaining in prayer. Yes, I had realized that I was attempting to control that which I could not and found myself in one big emotional jam. Music, I could still get lost in it and alcohol left the social world behind.

I was among co-workers who could not pick up on my telltale signs of my inner- child. Although, I was quite good at my craft-masking. I thought, we were doing nothing more than putting small Band-Aids on open wounds for the kids we served. And many inner-child's wounds had broken open and begun to fester. It was all overwhelming for me, this mixed batch of reality in my everyday life. Yet, when I was at work, I worked.

Oh, I lived God in my everyday life, so much conflicted then. I prayed tipsy, drunk; hungover, rolling out of the bed and sober too. I prayed for that hangover to stop hurting, pleading with God promising that I wouldn't do it again. I had long conversations with him of the negotiation type on my terms and conditions of course and my favorite asking for mercy I knew I didn't deserve it but that was the point, I had fun weekends. Yet, every night before going to bed, Monday through Thursday that was; I prayed, then I asked for understanding of myself, healing. I should have known it, temptation was coming I had made progress in my walk with God, despite my controlling ways. However, the test was always in the beginning of every temptation- a choice (God's part) and that part I was sadly not passing. Yet, this was nothing new, test and temptation were a part of everyday life. I tried to handle things on my own accord for the most part, but he was always there, my conscience could not deny it. God found me there in my trying times and things slowly stopped, my mask was off and the inner- child's sorrows were being addressed, what a mess, I thought, yet what a relief!

For years I tried to help the kiddos that we served within the confines of the established rules. It was forbidden to share the good news, so I had to be that role model and should be it every day. I had hoped that I had created opportunities during their struggles with their sorrows that would lead to healing and spiritual growth. I could imagine myself being them and them being me; we couldn't force change or growth, it was up to the individuals to fight hard for change, making wise decisions – choose (test) for the most part. God has his part too, of course. I had an "Aha" moment in which I realized that I was in the right place in my life and had stopped running away from the hurt this discovery was causing and my efforts to learn and heal were great. I thought that was cool! I could not change their past life events that led them to their circumstance, nor my own. I was thankful that the Lord provided the opportunities for me to explore my inner – child, opened up that bottomless pit! I, realizing I was not in control yet, felt that need to be in control, to feel safe. I was wrong; I needed Jesus, in Him I had in my sight the life God wanted for me.

1986

Suzie was a caregiver too. Not only for her grandson but for many people in the neighborhood. She helped those that were kicked around - swept under the carpet, you know the ones that society ignores. Suzie called them the underdogs; she had said like me. Like me, I thought, me as in herself or me. Nevertheless, I could recall how she would bring random homeless people to the house, allowed them to clean up, and gave them a meal. Suzie always had her big pot on the stove cooking soups. Its delightful aroma filled the air and with her homemade soup that had been served with the day-old bread from the bakery and a God Bless you to each person then she sat at her kitchen table. Suzie had her own little soup kitchen. It had started out with two people she had previously helped; they had come back to the house for something to eat and it had grown from there. Suzie had a good soul, I thought, God knew her best. Yet I have to admitted, sometimes I wished she would have seen me. And sometime I grew tired of all the people coming and going from the house. Between Suzie's friends, the donut – man (who I was too old to have funny games with any more) and the soup crew, I felt lost in the crowd. I knew it was a good thing to help people, but as a kid, I sometimes needed it to be just us, my crazy family in the house instead of the revolving door house.

Although, there was this one young guy who came to eat and would leave a dollar every time, even if he didn't care for the taste of the soup on a particular day. That young man never spoke a word and kept his head down low while he put his soup in his container, his bread he wrapped in a napkin then put both in his backpack and be on his way. Then one day he had raised his head and looked at Suzie and me, then told us,

"God bless you too".

Suzie served fifty families each year. I would sometimes help her; I'd drive her to the butcher shop to pick up turkeys for Thanksgiving and the hams for Christmas food baskets. I drove the family's station wagon to transport the turkeys, my car was a sports coupe. Suzie only drove a car once in her life and that was in the middle of a county road; using the center line as her guild to help her keep the car from leaving the road, she had told me. She was just too high-strung, but was great at giving orders.

"There's, a spot there, Jamie, oh you missed it; there, park here!" Suzie commanded.

She seemed always wound-up-tight until the project was done.

"We have to get some nice size turkeys, not the scrawny birds like you were, Jamie. You've filled out nicely, love your curvy waist. Last year they slipped four scrawny ones in the box, not this year, I'll make sure of that," she said in a matter-of-fact voice as we were walking from the car, parked in a Suzie approved parking space. Then we entered the red and white striped painted brick building with a ring from the cow bell attached to the top of the glass butcher shop door. It was quite busy that day being close to the holiday, there was at least ten customers in the small shop. I took a number while Suzie was checking out the sale items.

"Hey, Jamie, imagine all those squawking sound in the slaughterhouse while those dirty birds get their necks rung then hung upside down 'Woohoo" that's what they should have done to my uncle!" She exploded.

You could just imagine the people's reactions. Everyone took several steps back away from Suzie and me with their various strange and confused looks upon their faces. One guy had responded with a "what the hell"; and of course, Suzie gave the guy the same back. "What the hell!"

While other whispered among themselves, I was embarrassed, that was my usual response, and then aggravated. When they continued to stare with their glaring eyes focused on my blue-eyed soul. I became offended as they continued to look at Suzie as if she was a monster or something. It was over and I was not sure why they felt they had to continue to stare. So, I glared at them and asked if there was something, I could help them with, and if not, to please look away - happy holiday to yinz.

◊

One woman's food order was filled and as she was walking past Suzie whispered, "Get some help", then quickly exited the door with a ring of the bell as the door closed. Suzie stepped to go after the woman, but I stepped in front of her, leaned my face in by her ear and whispered, "Not today", stopping her before she had reached the door. ◊

Suzie was quite the fighter back in the day, and even though she was getting up in age, she would not hesitate to finish a verbal altercation with her fist. Besides, she knew she had back up. One story comes to mind when Suzie was in the yard enjoying the warmth of the summer evening breeze and the swishing of the rustling of the oak leaves on that big tree on that evening in July. She was relaxing on the glider; she was in her forties at the time. She had been watching Raymond worsh his car. Raymond was on the sidewalk at the side of the house and was just about finished worshing his car. A man drove by in a white four door car with a women passenger and she threw a cup of what seemed to be ice and pop, hitting Raymond's black convertible car on the hood. Raymond had yelled something directed at the driver and the driver of the white car stopped his car in the middle of the street, put it in reverse backing down the street. The scrawny young man leaned forward in his seat to see over the woman passenger, then the two exchanged words over the incident. The young guy, about the same age as Raymond, twenties at that time, put the car in park in the middle of the street at the demand of his woman passenger. Then a loud mouth, heavy set woman with a flowery pattern dress opened the car door, got out of the car walking over and stopped on the sidewalk directly in front of Raymond, informing him that she was going to hurt him if he said one more thing to her son. Suzie got up from the glider, walked over to the gate, opened it wide, and told Raymond to step in the yard and stand by her side. Suzie then informed the woman that if she thought she was big enough, laughing, to do something to her son, to please do so! Oh, why did she accept the dare? As soon as the flowered dress woman entered the yard and attempted to hit Raymond it was over before it begun. Suzie had punched the woman in her throat. The woman grabbed her throat, let out a screech clutching her throat in pain. Suzie then got a hold of the woman's brown hair pulling her downward towards the ground, knocking her off balance. And with one swoop of Suzie's right leg to the woman's left leg, the flowered dress lady went down. It looked like flowers were everywhere in the air then fell to the ground! Suzie kicked and stomped that woman what seemed like all over her body. Suzie was in her "red zone", that meant she had seen red and wanted blood. And indeed, that's what she got, blood! It took both Raymond and I to get Suzie away from the flower dress lady. Suzie pushed her out of the yard, the panic-stricken guy said nothing, simply collected her then placed her in the passenger seat of his car. Raymond generously closed the car door.

There was rumors in the neighborhood that the lady was beat up pretty bad and was in the hospital. Two months later there was a knock at the kitchen door; it was her, the flower dress lady, wearing a solid blue dress, Suzie's favorite color, holding flowers, colorful daisies in her hand apologizing to Suzie. She indicated she was out of line; she shouldn't have thrown the cup out the car window and would gladly pay for any damage that she may have had caused to the car. Although, it was quite difficult to understand her; with her jaw wired. Suzie had asked the woman if she knew who she was. The woman had indicated that she was informed of Suzie. Suzie was known in the neighborhood as a woman that took care of, and handle her business. That apologetic lady wasn't from the neighborhood and has never been seen again. I felt badly about the situation, and had hoped Suzie would have apologized too. I hope they moved on to bigger and better things in their life.

◊

Then I looked up at the "now serving" number and looked at the number on my slip, then thought it was going to be one of those days. Suzie was irritated and on a roll. Then all of the sudden Suzie was next; I thought "good looking out", God, then chuckled to myself. I smiled politely nodding my head in thanks because I knew we had the number eleven. I mouthed thank you to the Butcher and with boxes in hand and six other hands helping, we were out of there with a sendoff by the ringing of the cow bell, and we loaded the station wagon.

We were on our way to drop off those birds at the neighborhood Community Center, where Suzie was the volunteer vice President of the volunteer Human Services program. It had its perks. I thought I was dropping off Suzie too; instead, it seemed as Suzie had some free time before they got together to assemble the baskets. So, once the other volunteer had completed unloading the wagon, Suzie wanted to stay with me. She wasn't much of a people person; she kept her group interactions to a minimum. The others wanted her to stay and do lunch, but, no. However, I was proud of Suzie.

We were off to the thrift store, with one minor delay, I had to park the family station wagon at the house and get back into my car.

"To the thrift store, Jamie, and after that I'm buying us lunch!" Suzie said in a happy confident voice. I on the other hand, disliked thrift stores, they smelled like old stinky stuff and it was hard getting that smell out of my nostrils afterwards. But I tolerated it out of my love for Suzie. She enjoyed it so and could find some good stuff there, like curtains and drapes mostly, she had an eye for the length, width and inches and there were seventeen windows in the house. We had to go down every aisle of that big store that used to be a grocery store, and like a grocery, it was filled with items to buy. Whether she was interested in purchasing the item or not, she just had to look. I was more the get in, get what I needed, then get out type of shopper. Yet she did have a mission that afternoon, it was to buy baskets to be lined with plastic to place the Thanksgiving food items in it. She wasn't quite satisfied with the baskets they had. Baskets! I thought there were plenty of them in aisle two, I'd laughed to myself, but Suzie always had to go through the whole store. She ended up purchasing only two baskets and six sets of burgundy with gold paisley print drapes for the three living room windows. We had to skip lunch due to the lengthy stay in the stinky store. I dropped her off back at the center to her basket filling chore. Suzie embraced her caregiving role, which didn't stop at food baskets during the two holidays. I watched her walking toward the center's door, I called to her and she looked back at me. Her hand on the door, I told her that I loved her and was proud of her. I thought it was overdue and it was time to replace bad memories with some good ones. I thanked the Lord for Suzie.

I still attended church but did miss days due to my weekend drink-a-thons, yet I could say they were tapering off, Thank you Jesus! But not so much for Suzie. It was approaching spring and then summer, of course those were the seasons Suzie wore her many frowns. It was sad before Raymond left, but when he left it seemed to double. Nothing could compare to Raymond nor replace Raymond; Raymond was Suzie's forevermore. So, like the changing of the seasons in Pittsburgh – The Burgh, Suzie did too. She folded herself up within, meditating there in her yesterday world, there among Raymond's things and pictures, to only go through the seasons in a passive matter until seasons changed.

As a kid, Suzie would always make sure I gone to church even on those days when I believed I had enough people. I thought, and had told Suzie, that I was tired of their stares; I was just a kid. I wondered why they couldn't act like nice adults; they were in church; they could have saved their looks for after church was over. I even knew how to act; yes, I knew that there was a time and place for everything. I could hear Suzie snickering as she stood on the attic steps.

Then Suzie yelled, "The world would be a better place if it wasn't for the people Jamie! You're a part of people too, so get up and go to church, don't miss out on your chance to make a difference through your good actions. And if they look at you funny, just tell them you see them, but Jesus sees them too!"

Oh yeah, I got ready for church and had quite the time. I was watching the T.V. of life, took mental notes on which adults I was going to use the *I see you; Jesus sees you too* line on during the exchanging of the peace. I really didn't have to take too many notes; quiet as it kept. That was the time I received most of my glares, during the exchange of peace. I guessed I wasn't supposed to notice because I was just a kid, but I thought it was okay to do. I had Suzie's okay and it was wrong of them to look at me that way. And I was telling the truth- Jesus could see them; see us! Funny though, they didn't do it when Suzie was there. I had changed many faces that day: shocked faces, the" well-I never" looks, the surprised looks, indignant looks, and my favorite, the "excuse me" looks because it came with the question that meant I got to say it again. I got so carried away with it, I ended up saying it to everyone! Two people, one man and one woman had answered me by saying "that's right"; I thought that was cool. It was so, funny that after church Father had said he noticed that I seemed to be enjoying church that day. Yeah, Ha-ha, it is funny how somethings seemed to echo in the mind's eye but even sadder when it rang true so many years later.

So, I thought smiles, smiles; I would not be calling anyone on the looks I would receive. I made sure I had my protective mask on, not to be in my corrective mode. I did desperately want to belong. I thought about the saying "come as you are," then chuckled a little as I was walking into the church. I wondered if the church folks would let me in to the fold. Maybe, I thought, if I was them, they'd let me in. Sunday after Sunday after Sunday; it was the same thing; nothing changed. I tried to block it out, trying to focus on the sermon but it seemed liked they took turns. He or she would stare at me from a distance across the pews or one by one, some would even be turning around during the service looking back at me. I'd looked back with a smile on my face, and the responses were that I received a quite smirky smile or quick turns of the heads. I hung and shook my head, and every Sunday I managed to exit the church without incident, and was determine to continue to be in attendance. But the day did come when three fine church members, two women and one man, seemed to have gathered their unkind words to throw at me in a passive-aggressive mode. Oh, how they thought their words were clever. Yeah, I was watching the T.V. of life, I don't think I ever turned it off in my life or that I could. It could be a detriment at times or a very useful gift/tool. This was going to be one of those trying times for me, I could tell. But it was the scowls on their faces that were the telltale signs and turned me off. How could I convey to them that they were safe; I was at the house of God to seek Him? The line of questions was not welcoming; the what's, when's, where's and why questions regarding my life were simply design to discredit me or show that I had answered wrong as they took turns questioning me as if I was on a job interview. That I somehow needed their approval to attend. I was clearly not up to the standard of the "Elite Church Clique" and was given a rating of sorts which placed me in a category for a person they would exchange pleasantries with from time to time, if that. It was at that time "them" against "me", so it seemed.

I, on-the-other-hand, preferred what the Father had said over the elite clique's actions; he simply told me welcome home. I did like that; that was a heartfelt sincere welcome that had made me feel at home and want to stay home. But that experience was harmful to me, I had too much emotional and spiritual conflict to play church parishioner games. I was seeking myself, so that I could lose myself. I was in a fragile state. I only wanted to hear the sermon in hope that I could receive the good news and bring about change. Although, I knew it was nothing more than a mere distraction, but tell that to my hungry heart, I thought. The rank and file order for the members of the church meant so much to the elite. And I would have to contend with the T.V. of life reruns of their lack of kindness towards me from time to time; that was a detriment.

And unfortunately, their sly remarks and looks continued. I sat in my car after one service and thought: Rebellious, I thought, from the soles of their feet to the top of their heads. I thought the church community should be welcoming to all. They hugged even kissed me, then turned away talking rudely of me as if I was not there. Oh, these three, I thought sin was sin big or small just sin that was all- we're frail, fallen human beings should I be disliked because I sinned differently? Rebellious, there was a distinct odor of the inner-self could it have been rotten to the core? I thought!

Their misplaced concern with inconsistent hearts, my plea to God was that they troubled me no more. I watched the T.V. of life, my safety mechanism to keep me away from harm. I'd analyzed what was said in the manner of how it was said, watching their facial expressions - body language. A good tool if used right, but it could be disastrous if I wasn't looking through the right eyes. And I found myself mimicking their mannerism; supplying only one to two-word answers and attempted to keep my tone of voice pleasant; it was such a daunting task. One thing for certain, we all belonged to God; His beloved children. So, I prayed for myself, then the three that day, and then I wondered what could we have done to make things better. Oh, tenderheartedness I believed would have won.

So, I opted out of church for a while, I kept Jesus in the midst of my everyday life and over the years I struggled along the way and fell by the wayside. I was thankful, God continued to find me, and with him I was able to choose the road less traveled. It was a necessary time out of attending church. I was told by Suzie to attend church as a child, and after a brief discussion was encouraged by her as a young adult to leave the church and go live. I was then encouraged by her to return, and I returned and was so glad I did. You see, I'd thought during my time away from my church that the road to hell was paved with good intensions. That good acts/actions paved the road to salvation. I knew I had been wrong that either bad or good had nothing to do with my salvation; Jesus took care of that by ways of the cross. I had received my welcome home that time from all. I had realized that over the years Suzie had created opportunities for me that led me to accept the invitation to flourish in God's love.

1990

"When, does the party start Jamie," James inquired in a rather rough tone of voice

"You know you have to put the decoration up, get to it!" He yelled.

He didn't need the information and I didn't answer him. I continued gathering the bags of decorations off the kitchen table. The paper bags brushed against the skin of my arms which gave me a paper cut as I fumbled with them attempting not to drop any, to place them on the dining table while pushing my bucket of mop water to the side with my left foot. Catching the scented fragrance from the splash of suds I walked to the dining room, it smelled so fresh. Then I returned to the kitchen to mop, James was in a grumpy mood. I did, however, inform him I would need to mop the kitchen floor and that it would take 30 minutes to mop so I needed an hour for the floor to be done, nice and dry.

"Chill, I'll be back with Mom and Dad's anniversary cake in 45 minutes," he said.

It was the early 1990's, the World Wide Web hit; I had made my own hit then too. I was happy that my brother didn't live with our parents, yet he did from time to time. He had a good job driving trucks and lived with his girlfriend(s) and in between break ups would be back at home. There was too much for me to do then, I didn't need James' bad attitude. I was twenty-five years old during my parent's 41st Anniversary that year and the year was filled with a lot of last times for me.

I had heard James earlier that day, he had gone into his old bedroom. I heard laughter, not that of a hearty heartfelt kind of laugh. Then again, the type of laugh that was no laugh at all really coming out of anyone who lived in this house; that was for sure! No, this one had something hidden behind it. I knew that laugh, it was more like masking pain, pain that was filled with broken promises; broken dreams perhaps. That was the laugh. At least that's what it sounded like to me. Laughter beyond that closed bedroom door which quickly turned into an intense sobbing. I was only walking by. I had retrieved a tablecloth from the upstairs hall closet when I heard it all and then stood in astonishment as I was attempting to pass the door. But my feet just wouldn't more to get back to the dining room. I had never heard James cry. Yet, I did think that it was fitting – the heavy sobbing; it would be the type of cry he would have. I imagined James' contorted crying facial expressions and thought it would have looked like the opposite of his rage.

I had slowly backed away from the door, concentrated on my every movement placing my feet just so; I knew where the creaky hardwood was. I made four big intentional backward steps because I heard walking and what seemed like a throaty choking back tears sound following a hard-swallowing sound with a few sniffles, and then he sobbed. I thought salty tears, and continued walking backwards toward the closet. If I could make it back pass the closet, then I would go into the bathroom instead of attempting the creaky stairs that were too noisy. I kept my eyes wide open to be at the ready if I had seen James step out his door. A lump formed in my throat as I continued moving backward to reach the bathroom and heard the pounding beat of my heart, breathing through my mouth! I really didn't know why the lump had formed, please don't tell me that I was about to cry. I thought, maybe it was because James had been crying and I felt concerned for his suffering. Or was it merely fear of being caught by James there in the hallway outside the door. Yes, I'm sure of it, I heard his cry and it touched me so. I had found myself holding back the tears. I knew it only took one to fall to engage the rest and they would have come streaming down. But I had made it inside the bathroom without incident. I sat wanting for two minutes then went about my day.

It was not until about 5 o' clock that evening that I saw James again, right before I had to mop the kitchen floor, and it was a pretty good-sized floor. The vinyl fake brick rustic orange, brown and reddish looking floor that extended into the dining room stopped before the hard wood floor in the hall.

I had the music pumping and was in a dancing with the mop kind of rhythm. The floor required being mopped three times: the first pass was to remove the dirt with soapy suds, I used laundry detergent for that clean and fresh scent. The second pass was to remove the dirt and suds. The changing of the water was what I called the intermission to the dance, more like a required step in the mopping the floor process. It was the *bucket shuffle* down to the basement to dump and rinse the bucket out. Then the *add the water shuffle* with the mop dunk and twist. After the clean water shuffle, I would place the mop in the stationary tub and run the hot water on it while dunking it up and down until clean, water on cold then off, and twist. Then place the mop in the bucket and the slow drag up the basement steps for the rinse. I had made a left into the kitchen, but I would end my mopping in the small hallway right in front of the basement door. The third pass, I removed as much excess water as possible which led to the final step - the dry. I had the kitchen door opened wide as I started the third pass on the floor at the kitchen door to add to the drying phase. I had hoped James would be back at 6 o'clock. I thought I was the only one cleaning and had started yesterday, besides I only had those two lefts to do. Yet it should be alright, the party didn't start till seven. I had then started on decorating the dining room, right after I changed the C.D. and placed the C.D player on the chair. There was not much really:

I only had to place tape on the back of the homemade sign made on poster board then hang it on the wall, put the table pad and tablecloth on the table, set the table for buffet style dinning and blow up some balloons. However, my favorite song was on and I was lost in the song. I placed the gold pastel tablecloth on great grandma's beloved table. Although, it wasn't a 50th-wedding anniversary, that one was nine years away, it was the best tablecloth we had. Everything looked great, mainly the table, it was like a shrine to Mom but more like a dust magnet for me, but quite beautiful. I could understand it to a certain point, there were fond memories of it when Mom allowed it to be used. I took a trip down memory lane, God was good, I enjoyed those good times.

Then I was startled by thunder, immediately I turn off my C D player and clicked off the light, to both listen and be safe. Thanks to Mom, we were both afraid of thunder and lightning storms. And it rained and it rained hard that early evening as I watched from a distance. Pittsburgh's weather was known for its surprising weather flash thunderstorms, sometimes with hail, or in a blink of the eye a rainstorm with sun and rainbows, even chirping birds, and everything would then be dry in minutes. But this type of rain had made mud that ran down from the garden area in the yard onto the cobbled stone ground. Although, it was a quick torrential downpour, it was the kind that rained hard so fast that if someone was caught out in its James would be soaked in about three seconds - type of rain and I hoped James was dry.

And with the slamming shut of the screen door and stomping in place sounds of what sound like heavy work boots, I knew James had returned. This was followed by a short walk across the floor, it seemed like the walking stopped at the table. I on the other hand stopped in my tracks, closed my eyes and sighed. It didn't matter anymore if the floor had dried, but it wasn't.

"What the hell, Jamie, this floor is still wet!" James yelled in a sharp loud voice. I stepped into the kitchen and was quite upset; it was as I had imagined.

I told you the floor needed 30 minutes to dry and you should have come back at six! I don't have the time to clean up after you, James; those big spot of mud and tracks you made. I didn't have time for that mess. I needed to finish with the decorations.

I told James he would have to mop it up.

"What did you say? You told me to do what?" he asked.

I told him again to clean it!

"That's, what I thought you said," he replied in a calm voice. I was turning to leave the kitchen then, *wham*, a right hook to my left ear! I felt the pain and heard the sound made by the cartilage at the outer curvy part of my ear, up from the earlobe as it broke. Something like rough sandpaper being torn or the sound of the cartilage in the knee or shoulder that had rubbed together as a person, moved about; that sound. I hit James back! For the first time in my life. I turned around and hit James hard with a left jab to his face! Oh, and I was a fighter too, you had to be in my neighborhood and as you know I had learned at a young age. But I wasn't a bully like James and had not had to fight in years. But it appeared I had had enough of James! It was so much of a spontaneous reaction – a release of free energy. I had no time to think; I couldn't turn the other cheek! James took care of the cheek part in his way as he followed up with another hit, only this time harder that turned my cheek for me. The hit knocked me off balance, it landed in the same place at the ear but cupped my ear, and my ear rang. I had shaken my head quite hard, after I grabbed with my right hand and held on to the kitchen sink to steady myself, my left hand at my left ear of course. And I was leaning on the sink cabinet on my left side not to fall, I did not dare fall. I could not go down, anyone who was a true street fighter knew that!

"What, the hell is your problem Jamie?" James asked, then held his stomach and laughed loud and harshly, but it had been hard for me to hear; I barely heard it over the ringing in my ear.

"I give it to you, that was a good hit, but I advise you not to try that ever again!" he indicated to me through his teeth.

"Ever!" he yelled.

He put his face in my face with his head slightly tilted to the left side so he could be eye to eye with me, his Greek looking nose smashing into my snub nose to emphasize his point. That was the last time I hit James.

"I'll, clean up the floor, not because you told me, but because company will be coming soon!" he informed.

I left the kitchen still dazed, in pain, and somewhat concerned about my condition and went to my room to lie down. I was completely out for some time, only to be woken by hearing a male with a husky sounding voice who called to me to come down, that it was time to cut the cake, so I went. I couldn't recall what time it was but it had been dark out then. I had come back around, Dad had sometimes said that I had a hard head, and I thought this time it was good to have one even though he wasn't referring that type of hard. And before I had called it a night, I tried to mend the cartilage to the upper outer curved part of my ear by placing toilet paper up and under it. I attempted to line the two pieces together, hoping it would mend itself, I didn't know it wouldn't work.

And before that night had come to its end, I had found out I had forgot to put the table pad on the table, and there was a ring on it. Mom pointed down at it and she was pissed. She told me James was moving back in and she thought my room would be the best for him. And that way, his bedroom could be used for when there was company.

"And, after what you did to my table, Jamie, that puts you out!" Mom bellowed, "Thanks for the anniversary gift, Jamie!"

I looked at Mom and told her that I was sorry, to please forgive me. Then I had said okay and had asked if I could get some clothes from the room. She nodded her head yes even so slightly; the look on her face was one of those Mother's looks that spelled disaster if I didn't hurry up and remove myself from her sight, I thought yes, it was time to go. That was my last night living at the house, and the last time the cartilage in my ear was whole. Dear God, I thought I was sad, sad we treated one another that way. And wondered if James had been his ideal to take my room that lead to Mom's decision, he was her baby boy and she favored the boys.

James had so much sorrow, so much fury because of his sorrow's woes it was too much for him to bear, nor could I bear it anymore. It had seemed he had no one to talk to unless he had it all bottled up inside and it was seeping out exploding on unsuspecting people, James knowing of the true nature of his outburst or not. I could relate to the brutality and was at work on my own issues. His girlfriend had had enough of his negative attitude and had called it quits, which explained his sobbing. I guessed James had experienced at least two or more of *last times in his life* too that day. I hoped for the best for James and forgave him, but I knew it was better for me to stay away from him as much as possible; it was beneficial for my health.

But everywhere James went, he made friends and was loved. His personality was similar to that of our Dad's; minus the terrible rage he displayed at times. James could talk to anyone by being so funny; a joker. Most of his friends would pay him compliments and tell him he should be a comic; an all-around funny guy, they had said. But we all knew guys that used humor to hide their sadness, pain; despair.

Yeah, James had his mask on too. He being a joker, coupled with his outburst told of the story behind the mask. Any set of caring eyes could see it, if they just looked. It was a whole other story to help someone heal, if you know what I mean. For the most part, he could be cool, laid-back, that was the part that was like Dad; yet, I had believed his cool and laid-back self was on the surface. And for some guys it was the part of the attraction; they knew he could play some mean football and it was great to be in his company if any trouble broke out after the games, or at the bar; woe to those who crossed him.

We shared common friends and could be in one another's company at times. But that didn't stop James from taunting me from time to time; he set his sight on me and I would become the brunt of his jokes then. I had to fully put my mask on and I laughed to get along. Some of the guys, mostly Fred didn't find the jokes quite funny and would reprimand James, told him it wasn't funny - not cool, that I was his sister; put him on the spot to be cool and James would play it off. Only after, he gave me his dagger eyes every chance he could, but always told me jokingly that he was only playing round. I had made my peace with James. I was good. And over the years mutual friends had faded away, and so did I. I did, however, maintain two friends from back in the day. I had made my choice; I felt I was needed elsewhere, and moved on.

Time marched on, I found myself far away from the world I used to live in due to who I had chosen. I found it hard at time; but of course, to walk the road less traveled with so many choices in the world it wasn't easy. I had become overwhelmed by the visual aid of the things the world had to offer, consuming goods and services, lacking in moderation. It was consuming me to no end, I had thought, until my focus was restored. God called me back and I was emerged in His truth. I needed those distractions at times. I guessed they were necessities that moved me away from, yet not too far; that lead me to a void in need of the truth which comes into view. I was quite a hard headed person, who more than likely had to learn the hard way; but not always, hence the strengthening in my everyday walk in life with God amongst the worldly choices. I knew I couldn't do it myself; life's paths would not be clear. Yet, I carried on with the knowledge that I was not alone, overwhelmed or not. I remained, therefore, consuming the wine, consuming the bread amidst the struggle of life. I had to release all that which overwhelmed me into His hands, and to allow my Lord to take the lead placing all others and worldly thing below Him, they were mere possessions. This in and of its self I could not complete without God.

James had found a girl who was more than happy to stand by his side. She had seen through his mask, and I found myself in attendance at their wedding, a small but elegant wedding. She had reached James, and as the years went by the little ones came into view. Years after the kiddos, the divorce had occurred and James was a bachelor. Yet, he too was not alone and he had picked up the bible, Jennifer reported, and he was doing well. I kept him in prayer. It seemed like I always had; as I did for all my siblings. God was indeed good to us. For I did not live my calamity alone, we simply had different experiences in our common dysfunctional roots. I think people would say we were lucky to survive: but I would beg to differ because God was there. We got together from time to time, and Jennifer was working on plans for a visit; she was good at taking charge and being organized regarding gatherings. I waited for her call.

I had felt mentally and physically ill an hour or so before I received my sister's call. I was in the company of others at lunch, yet felt an overwhelming sense of loneliness, as if a heavy wet blanket had been draped over my shoulders, and I became cold. Some had noticed a strange look upon my face, I suppose, I was unaware, and they had inquired to my well- being. I had informed them that all was well, and thanked them for their concern, then excused myself from their company returning to the office in a perplexed state of mind. I did not feel ill in the sense that required medical care, I thought; yet, there it was, that pain I felt in the pit of my guts that seemingly made its way about my chest. Perhaps I had ate something that simply didn't agree with me; yes, surely that was it, I thought. However, that did not take into account why I felt a feeling of loss- separation. I sat there at my desk, then called a few people inquiring about their day and well-being. But it turned out that they had become concerned about mine. And yet again, I had informed those that I spoke to that I was well, ending all three calls I had placed on a reassuring note.

Then walking down the hallway, I entered the restroom. I speculated if I put cold water on my face the water would somehow refresh me making it better. I had asked God what could this be. Why did I feel such a way? I prayed that it would soon pass. Stepping out of the restroom my cell phone vibrated within my left pants pocket and stopped me in my tracks. Reaching in my pocket to retrieve my phone, flipping it open, then pushing the little green picture of the phone button activating the call and said hello. It was Jennifer, I could hear the surprising shock in her voice yet could not imagine anything.

Jennifer inquired, "Are you sitting down, Jamie?"

I informed her I was not, but was standing and pleaded for her to inform me of the news.

"You, may want to sit before I tell you what happened, Jamie," Jennifer whimpered "James died; he's died!"

I shrieked at the top of my voice "What?" which of course drew attention to me. I started pacing the hallway floor questioning her with what seemed like every unstable step I took. You know, the what, when, where and how of it all. My head hung low, I had kept it there purposely and had raised my right arm and index finger to both acknowledge the co-worker's presence and to indicate that I needed a moment while walking away. I tried to comfort Jennifer, which was impossible as I knew she would cry uncontrollably for quite some time; she was the sensitive one, so we ended the call.

And in all my walking back and forth I had found myself outside, I stood there on the side walk, wondering why? Unaware that the emotions and pain I felt earlier were not upon me anymore. I fondly recalled the day of the ride to work those many years ago and could see James there in his truck; smiling – smiled at me. It was love I thought, the reason that James took me to work that day! Having placed my right hand over my heart feeling its beat for a moment as James' heart had stopped; the cause for the reason James had to leave, so they said. I knew who was in control, and who called him home. I had asked the Lord to forgive James and rest his soul, but I quickly thought I didn't need to ask for forgiveness for James. About two years back we had all got together and James had announced he had accepted the Lord Jesus Christ as his personal savior. And as I continued to stand there, I noticed the sky was blue and nature was in bloom. Ah yes, a new being I thought, then smiled. I raised my left arm from the elbow up – slightly tilted towards the sky palm open and held it there... I waved goodbye. It had been the spring of 1996 when James said his goodbye. Tears formed in my big bark brown soulful eyes, but not one fell; I did not cry.

2000

It was the year 2000, the end of the first 2000 years had been reached. When an unforeseen noise came from the kitchen that startled me during my morning meditation and I had gone to the kitchen to locate its source. The interference was generated by none other than Suzie who was awake fairly early that morning, the sun had not raised. She was attempting to make morning tea, and the interference would grow into something I should not speak of. But I recalled the windows were closed and on that sunny morning, sunshine came in through the open top shutters of the windows, with the drapes and curtains drawn to each side. Sometimes through the spaces, in between the closed shutters, when the drapes and curtains were drawn to each sides of the windows of that old Victorian house, the sun came through. Suzie had a variety of ways to showcase the windows of the house. And not much had changed, other than the changing of the drapes and the curtains in the kitchen and bathroom as the seasons changed. There was a fresh coat of paint to the walls at times to enhance the physical appearance of the house; it was in a polished, rustic, clean state.

I watched Suzie as I stood there leaning on edge of the wall next to the phone and light switch. Suzie was walking slowly with a slight shuffle to her stride, in black house shoes and a blue dress, her favorite color. I turned on the light with a flick of the finger; Suzie looked up and continued on. Her hour-glass shape was since long gone; filled in over the years, and she had some health issues in her declining years. She reached the stove, reaching for the rooster painted red kettle, sounding off its whistle as the water came to a boil. Although, her attractiveness remained only slightly hidden by the lines on her worn face, still, I could see her there. She moved slowly towards the table with that rooster painted red kettle in her right hand, a hand that was wrinkled and trembled a little, then stopped once she reached the table. Yet, she had left the gas stove burner top on. She was pouring the hot water from the rooster kettle into her cup, but without a tea bag in her cup, she usually placed it in beforehand. Her steel blue eyes dulled in color and sight; the water flowed over the cup's edge onto the table, then spilled on the floor. She was flustered and quickly put the kettle on the sink counter; her eyes widened with an intense emotion of fear displayed there within her eyes and an alarming look on her face as I walked into her view."What's your name?" Suzie asked in a puzzling matter

"Oh help me, I made a mess!" She stood by the sink's edge moving her arms about in a frantic manner. I told Suzie it was okay, then told her my name; yet, *what's your name* stepped in to assist, cleaning the mess. Then I gave Suzie her tea and some eggs to eat. I turned off the fire to the stove after I had cooked the eggs. Suzie had simply left it on for me, that's all. She sat in her seat only after I had cooked the eggs, the aroma made me a bit hungry and I wanted two of my own after Suzie settled in, but she was rather frustrated. Poking at her eggs curiously, looking down, and in her cup of tea. She glared at me through those eyes of hers, inquiring doubt; eyes that were very much a part of her strength.

"Poison, Poison! Why are you trying to kill me?" Suzie shouted at me with what seemed like at the top of her voice. Oh Suzie, I had informed her it was me; I would not harm you. Yet I remained nameless. She would have no parts in what I had to say, and pushed the plate of eggs aside bumping it into the cup, splashing tea up into the air which fell onto her plate of eggs, and there on the table too.

She got up from her chair and began to pace the floor, all the while keeping an eye on me.

"There, you can clean up that mess too since you're so good at cleaning mess and trying to poison me!" She directed.

I used a napkin dabbing up the tea off of the eggs and placed the plate back in front of Suzie's chair, and refreshed her tea. She feared me, and I couldn't understand why. Yet she eventually joined me back at the breakfast table. I did manage to get some drink and food in her by engaging her in a happy story from her past. She seemed to prefer those conversations over the present ones; time had passed. I thought it best we should depart from the kitchen. Suzie walked a fearful walk, real or imagined, and mine was a puzzled walk, as we walked across the kitchen floor. At one point that puzzled look showed on my face, and I had thought I had changed my look before Suzie had seen it, but it was too late.

We were in the small hall by the basement door when Suzie noticed the look. She stopped from going any further by placing her right hand on the basement door knob and held onto her right wrist she was quite strong.

Suzie asked frightfully, "Where are you trying to take me? I didn't want to go down there."

Suzie feared me, this no named stranger who attempted to kill her with poison was escorting her somewhere she did not want to go; so, Suzie must have thought, my heart felt her fright. I had informed her of the location once again, yet her fearfulness increased. She reluctantly moved on only after a great deal of time had gone by and it was quite the task. She lumbered clumsily with every step she took. At times appearing as if she were to fall. I would reach out to her aid only for her to take several steps back to avoid my touch, while staring angrily at me.

We had made it to the dining room with another stop at the mantle.

"Oh, look at that pretty blue candle, I remember the day I got it," She beamed and proceeded to tell the story. I had replied with an "Aha" here and there as she picked the candle up for a closer look. I took a deep breath in, and had slowly let it out; it was such a long story then. I had told Suzie that there were more candles she could see, to come on in a rather sweet tone of voice, then smile. She placed the candle back on the mantle and we walked on, and I had hoped out of the dining room.

"Where am I going?" Suzie asked, "I want to be left alone," pulling her right foot back from mid step, away from the hardwood hallway floor, then planted it firmly down onto the dining room vinyl floor with a furious look in her eyes and face. I had cringed, then thought yet again, a stop, this time stopping at the edge where the dining room vinyl floor ended and the hallway hardwood floor began. A stop in each new section of the house, I thought. It appeared as if time stood still, there was nothing more in life to do but what we were doing at the command of Suzie's sudden change of emotions - of her mind set. We stood there at times, both of us shifting our hips from one side to the other; I placed my hands on my hips at times too. Suzie didn't care for it, and I knew it, but I did it anyway so she could share in my aggravation too. I speculated the cause, but it remained unexplained to me, why she wouldn't move on. And then at that point, I struggled with my own emotions too.

I wasn't sure what I said or did, if anything, or what Suzie had determined that changed her mind, but after a great deal of my pleading and the power she had over me, our feet touched down onto the hardwood hall floor. We continued our walk through the hall; Ha-Ha, about sixteen steps, thirty-two if you combined the steps between the two of us together, yet I felt hopeful. My focus was placed on the number of steps as a distraction from Suzie's behavior. It was sporadic, at best, changing from fearful to angry, crying then to being somewhat cheerful. It kept me humble.

Then a right turn through the wide opened double doors, and we were there. I sighed a sigh of weary relief looking upward then reflected a *Woo* to God.

"Oh, look at the beautiful blue candles on the mantle, oh and the gray elephants, there's a mommy, daddy and a baby one. Ha-Ha, the baby one is me!" Suzie said with excitement in her voice while she rushed over to the beautiful grayish white marble mantelpiece fireplace in the living room for a closer look. I always thought the baby elephant represented Raymond, at least that's how I remembered it being told. They were some of her favorited knick-knacks, and there were two blue sets of tapered candle sticks in clear holders, six in all. Suzie placed them at the opposite ends of the mantle. The three in each set, Suze had said, represented the Father, Son and the Holy Ghost. And the elephant family, with their trunks up for luck, were placed in the center. To the right was a picture of Raymond, and to the left, one of Suzie's husband. I had turned on the T.V. and found some old familiar show, and Suzie sat on the charcoaled gray color love-set watching it from there.

"It's chilly, make a fire, would you?" Suzie asked with a suspicious smirk, lips tightly closed and cocked to the right side, rolling her eyes at me. I had replied with a quick yep. I looked up at the side window and the top shutters were opened, the burgundy with gold paisley printed drapes were drawn to each side of the window. I thought for a moment to draw the drapes, but knew the two front windows were in the same position. There were beams of light that shined through the closed bottom shutter's openings at the front windows. If I would have made a change to one window, I would have had to change them all. Suzie was meticulous about the house windows being in suit with one another, and there were seventeen of them. The middle size fire was lit, and started a slow steady burn.

Then I stepped out of the living room and was back with a sammitch and a cup of tea for lunch. I kept my head down, eyes low, and remained silent when I placed Suzie's lunch on the small table tray and put it in front of her. Then I sat in the nearby burgundy recliner chair, and thought it odd since Suzie usually sat in that chair. Although, I didn't give it another thought as I enjoyed the crackling sound of the burning wood fire and its orange glow. While Suzie drank her tea, and ate her corned beef sammitch on rye, and took a small bite of her sliced kosher dill pickle, I chuckled to myself, even though its "poison". Suzie ate as if the poison incident didn't occur at all. She then made a motion as if she was going to put the pickle back on her plate, but instead raised it to her nose, closed her eyes, and breathe deeply in, smelling it. I braced myself when she opened her eyes and made eye contact with me.

"I love, the smell of pickles, it reminds me of the big pickle barrels in the store Grandma used to take me, my sister, and my brother to," She cheered; I exhaled in relief, and thought I really had to work on my sarcastic ways, even when it was just a thought. It was turning out to be a pleasant afternoon experience, compared to the early morning start. I speculated that maybe Suzie just didn't get enough sleep that night; that caused her to be disorientated, that was all, but I did hold some concerns. Unfortunately, those steel blue eyes of hers stared into the fire, then with a quick turn of her head, her eyes fell on me; the T.V. program amused her no more. She locked eyes with me, a panicked look on her face; I don't know her, she must have thought. Who was this stranger that followed me from room to room? She slowly moved the tray table to her left side looking down at times at the tray. While she was moving it to the side, she kept an eye on me too. Then she sprung up from that old love-set, stood there close to me. Those eyes of her glaring down, and she gave me such a dirty look. She was known to be able to look at someone and make that person feel too small or unimportant to be worthy of her consideration. I could attest, I felt unworthy quite often. I pushed back in the chair, almost reclining it back, and quickly sat up and stopped the recliner. I was on pins and needles. I kept my eyes on Suzie too, I was not sure what would come next, but hoped for the best.

"Who, are you? What's your name?" Suzie questioned me in a harsh manner. "Why are you here?"

I told Suzie my name and before I could response any further...

She replied in a demanding tone of voice, "Jamie? I don't know anyone named Jamie, you stay here whoever you are; stay here, I'm going up to my bedroom!" she said.

She walked past me, past the old maple center table, then the couch and out of the living room's opened double doors, stopping in the hallway, turning ever so slightly, then looking at me with a look on her face as if she dared me to move.

"I'm tired. I'm going to lay down, if you don't mind; you're welcome to stay down here!" She instructed me loudly. Her demands were received loud and clear as I remained seated, and in a concerned state. I watched her, every bend at her knees; listened to every stomp and creaking sound of steps with each step she took. "I'm tired. I'm going to lay down, if you don't mind; you're welcome to stay down here!" She instructed me loudly. Her demands were received loud and clear as I remained seated, and in a concerned state. I watched her, every bend at her knees; listened to every stomp and creaking sound of steps with each step she took. "I'm tired. I'm going to lay down, if you don't mind; you're welcome to stay down here!" She instructed me loudly. Her demands were received loud and clear as I remained seated, and in a concerned state. I watched her, every bend at her knees; listened to every stomp and creaking sound of steps with each step she took. "I'm tired. I'm going to lay down, if you don't mind; you're welcome to stay down here!" She instructed me loudly. Her demands were received loud and clear as I remained seated, and in a concerned state. I watched her, every bend at her knees; listened to every stomp and creaking sound of steps with each step she took.

She sometime paused, stopping to look at me, then continued on till we could not see one another anymore. I heard her walk the short hallway to the bathroom, then the bedroom door being closed with a slight bang. I exhaled and put my pins and needles to rest. Still I wondered about the sudden onset of increase anger and so much confusion. Why Suzie was acting so strangely? What had set her off? Her doctor's office wasn't open on Saturdays, but I could call my concerns in for a Monday review. We were on our own God, Suzie and me. I thought back on the morning's events in hope of pin-pointing the problem. It was 3:00 P.M., the fire was nothing more than a smoldering flame as I sat and pondered what it could be while dialing the phone. I had asked the Lord to help Suzie, to help me as I listened to the phone ring waiting for the recorded message to pick up my call. It felt like only a few minutes went by when I heard Suzie yelling, then a loud thump. It was so alarming; I had been in deep thought. I quickly hung up the phone without a word spoken. I jump out of the chair, yelled up to Suzie inquiring if she was alright, then I was on my way.

There I was; I opened the door wide and stood in the doorway of Suzie's bedroom. I looked to the right, there she sat on the right side of her bed, her back towards me. I had asked if she was okay and received a nod of her head as a response. I looked around the room that belonged to ancient times. There were black and white photos displayed in ornate picture frames of Suzie's siblings and one photo of my Mom. An old fashion powder makeup box and old perfume bottles with that all too There I was; I opened the door wide and stood in the doorway of Suzie's bedroom. I looked to the right, there she sat on the right side of her bed, her back towards me. I had asked if she was okay and received a nod of her head as a response. I looked around the room that belonged to ancient times. There were black and white photos displayed in ornate picture frames of Suzie's siblings and one photo of my Mom. An old fashion powder makeup box and old perfume bottles with that all too There I was; I opened the door wide and stood in the doorway of Suzie's bedroom. I looked to the right, there she sat on the right side of her bed, her back towards me. I had asked if she was okay and received a nod of her head as a response. I looked around the room that belonged to ancient times. There were black and white photos displayed in ornate picture frames of Suzie's siblings and one photo of my Mom. An old fashion powder makeup box and old perfume bottles with that all too There I was; I opened the door wide and stood in the doorway of Suzie's bedroom. I looked to the right, there she sat on the right side of her bed, her back towards me. I had asked if she was okay and received a nod of her head as a response. I looked around the room that belonged to ancient times. There were black and white photos displayed in ornate picture frames of Suzie's siblings and one photo of my Mom. An old fashion powder makeup box and old perfume bottles with that all too familiar smell that was bothersome to me were about the room. All were displayed on the three vintage dressers and two matching nightstands along with other things. My eyes fell upon the knick-knacks and more photos of people of lost times adorning the off-white mantled fireplace. Things looked to be in order, then I noticed the sun light that filled the room that came from the two front windows, I had thought the ceiling light was on. The light blue drapes were tucked behind the upper and lower sets of shutters and the windows were closed. I knew then something indeed was wrong with Suzie.

I stepped into Suzie's room walking toward the right of the room towards her bed, then stopped dead in my tracks. I looked down at the navy-blue wall-to-wall carpeted floor for a better look and I saw two objects under the bed. My eyes widened with shock; my mouth dropped! I asked Suzie what she had done.

"There they are, they're together!" Suzie said in a calm but eerie voice.

I didn't bother to look up as I was taking a closer look. I was in awe of what I had seen and therefore, was at a loss for words, remaining silent. There scatted about that navy- blue carpet grayish, heavily in some spots, ashes- Human Cremated Remains; those of her husband and of her son! Their urns were on the floor halfway under Suzie's bed in an attempt most likely to conceal them I guessed. I was bewildered. Dear God, what was I to do? I looked up at Suzie, she had been still sitting there yet restlessly moving about with her back towards me, which I thought was strange. So, I tiptoed around to the right side of her bed carefully concentrating on my every move, passing the dresser that was tucked against the pale blue wall beside the mantel piece. My actions had a rather ghostly reminder of having to step lightly before. But then I had to dodge back to the right so not to step on a heavily grayish ashes spot on the other wise plush navy-blue carpet, so soft to the touch. However, it placed me right in front of Suzie, and I looked at her, then gasped

Human Cremated Remains – ashes on Suzie's hands, her clothing, face and on and in her mouth! Suzie had consumed human remains! I wondered what parts and who's? Totally insane, wasn't it. Then I questioned Suzie as to why?

"I wanted them to be a part of me!" She muffled as a clump of saliva filled ashes fell out of Suzie's mouth. She patted her lap and located the broken clump of ash. I believed we were both frantic then. I hovered over Suzie, I tried to get to those hands, get to that mouth, to stop her as she was in the process of putting her closed left hand into her mouth! I had asked her to open her mouth, she shook her head angrily. And she pulled away from me; I missed catching her hand - too late, it was in her mouth! I got a hold of and I held onto Suzie's left wrist, while her hand was still in her mouth. Her jaw was in motion and she attempted to swallow. I was busy about wiping away what remained of those remains from Suzie's face and hand with my bare hand, and I was able to move her hand away from her mouth. Then I wiped her clenched mouth and chipmunk looking cheeks! She swung hitting me in the face, arm and back. While I was gripping the sides of her cheeks with my thumb and fingers slightly pressed into both sides of her jaw, I told her with great force in my voice to open her mouth up and stick out her tongue. She did as I asked. I quickly wiped her tongue off with my right hand and felt a gritty spongy feeling on the palm of my hand as I pressed down on her tongue. I then did a fast-hooked pinky finger sweep and hoped she wouldn't bit down. Gritty ash had made its way under my finger nail, yet I was able to remove a good amount of clumpy moist ash from her mouth.

"Stop, Stop, turn me loose!" Suzie demanded of me. It was what seemed like a hostile stare down, and I broke off the eye contact. Besides, I couldn't compete with those steel blue sarcastic eyes. She hit me, and I let go of her arm not to escalate the situation any farther. Time seemed to linger on-and-on, move on I prayed, as I stood there in front of Suzie. I looked at the clock radio on the nightstand beside Suzie's bed, it was 6:46 p.m. I thought it was much later. While Suzie attempted to put her hand back in her mouth, in a stern matter-of-fact voice I told Suzie she had to stop, no more eating the ashes, and no more hitting.

Then in a child-like, subtle voice she answered me, “Okay, Mum I’ll be good – I’ll be a good girl Mum!”

I was amazed Suzie stopped. I stepped back, having to move to my left toward the side window out of some ashes. Suzie wiped her hair from her face, then wiped her moist hands off on the sides of her blue dress leaving smeared marks on both sides. She then placed her arms to her sides raising them both from the elbows up and brought her hands together. That was when I could see the ashes in between her fingers as she interlocked them one to the other, folding them down, then placing her folded hands on her lap. Suzie, my blue-eyed soul, turned her head to the left and looked at me, so removed from it all. We looked at each other. I didn’t know this person; the Suzie I’d known wasn’t present then as she gazed into my eyes in a docile childlike manner. This Suzie began to cry in silence, some tears ran down her right cheek forming an ash-filled tear. The sight of it changed my mood and I thought how *tragically beautiful*. I was no longer a *stranger*; I had become Suzie’s Mother. So, I played the role of what I thought a Mother was supposed to be. I went back to her, wiped the tears away, and then hugged Suzie, remains and all. She melted into my arms placing her cheek on my left breast, resting there. Her arms were no longer at her side anymore but round my waist as she held on tight, and she had a good cry. I held her closer and remained quiet and void of thought. She whispered in a cracked tiny voice that she felt and heard my heart. Upon hearing this I melted into the embrace as I pulled her closer and said Dear God! We had quite a bit of ashes on us, but I had become more concerned about Suzie’s well-being then the ashes. In fact, I didn’t look down to watch my step when I walked over to her again. It had been a long time since I wondered about whose remains were whose, and whose and what parts had been consumed. However, I did want to clear all the ashes from Suzie's mouth, off of her and off of me. I informed Suzie of my intentions after a while, then I released her from the embrace.

I stepped out of the bedroom, went into the bathroom, turned on the cold water for a glass of water for Suzie. I got the glass, red bucket and some peach colored warsh rags (washcloths) from under the sink's cabinet as my intention was for Suzie to rinse her mouth out then spit into the bucket. After I placed the filled glass of water on the side of the sink, I turn on the hot water adding it to the cold and wet two warsh rags, setting one to the side of the sink while washing my hands. At a glance I saw my face in the medicine cabinet mirror then frantically washed the gritty ash off my face. I was caught up in the moment of wiping all over myself and had to refocus to return to Suzie. So, I quickly rinsed the wash cloth and sadly watched the watery ash go down the drain.

I reentered the bed room, flicking the light switch on with my left pinky finger which turned on the center ceiling light to the room. Then I had to immediately place the glass of water on the night stand, the bucket on the floor, and yet keep the warsh rag in my hand. There Suzie stood, facing me, holding an urn in front of her body with both hands. Her arms stretched out in front of her, then in a swift upward motion raised the dark brown open urn up into the air releasing the ash-gray cremated human remains like confetti that seemed to go everywhere.

Suzie proclaimed, “Be, Free! I needed to set him free! How would you like it to be stuck in there? Get out of my room!” She then bent down placing the urn on the floor and made the attempt to get the other urn. I jumped on the bed, rolling to the right side where Suzie was. My actions must have startled her because she stopped, then stood up from the bent over position. I got up from the bed and stood between her and the urn. She made several attempts to reach between my legs and tried to maneuver around me to reach the urn. I shifted my body parts accordingly and blocked her every move, it must have looked like a crazy dance if we had had an on looker or music was playing at the time. I informed Suzie that despite her every effort she would not accomplish her goal. Then she lunged at me, toppling me onto her bed, as she wickedly laughed. I countered with a, “what the hell, Suzie!”

"That's what you get!" She said as I rolled over, then over once more getting off of the bed. I swiftly walked past the mantle, leaving the warsh rag behind on the bed, to the dresser. I made my way to the dresser wondering what triggered the disturbance that caused Suzie to scatter the human remains of her husband or son about like confetti. Why had she felt the need to consume and free the remains? And, yes, why had she called me Mum? Yet, I was not alone in my walk, I reached the dresser and turned sideways towards Suzie. I then watched Suzie as she walked towards me with what seemed like great intent to do me harm, tramping the ashes under her bare feet. She looked down at her feet, then looked back up at me with such disgust displayed in those eyes of hers and upon her face. I had no doubt that her strong disapproved reaction was aroused by me.

"Look, what you made me do! You can just leave that vest thing in the dresser I won't let you put it on me!" She asserted in a loud forceful manner as she continued to walk towards me. Okay, I thought, she hasn't lost her mind completely, but braced myself for what would come next. She turned and went back to the ash side of the room, picking up the other urn off the floor, held the dark brown open container close to her breast as in an embrace, then made a swift upward motion and yet again gray ash cremated human remains rained down, this time on her, the bed, chair, night stand and of course the floor. Suzie had indeed accomplished her twisted goal. She had released them both from their confinements--freed them both. And for a moment, she wore a satisfied look within those eyes of hers and what looked like a content grin on her mouth as she stood there clothed in ash, looking at me from across the room. But I sensed she wasn't quite done with me.

"Ha-Ha-Ha, there I freed them," She proclaimed then came charging at me.

I informed Suzie it would be best if she would calm down.

"Calm down, calm down?" Suzie said, "I'm just getting started." Suzie then kicked, pulled at me, and struck me on my face, arms, sides; pretty much all over my body, ashes going everywhere. She was much taller than I. I was only 5' 4, so she had advantage over me. Heck, she was like a human windmill, her wheeling arms and fists hitting me one after the other in her deliberate intent. Although, I had endured much more than that, so I let her have at it for a moment. I opened the top dresser drawer and reached in with my left hand pulling out the safety restraint kit. It was bagged in clear plastic like a dry-cleaner's see-through plastic. While attempting to hold her way from me with my right hand, her hits became harder in her fury. How clever her mind was even in that disturbed state? It appeared to have been engaged like in her normal function, but now her mind was being used to her dysfunctional advantage to get things she wanted done. What a wonderfully crafted mind God has made, I thought. I had truly underestimated the extent of her condition. But I had managed somehow to open and remove the vest, extension straps and only one of the hand mittens. Suzie promptly grabbed the mitten, then threw it across the room, landing in the sitting area towards the front of her bed room. I used that action as a way to get away from Suzie, and walked quickly towards the left side of the bed to the nightstand. I looked across the bed to the nightstand on the right of the bed to note the time, it was only 9:36 p.m. I thought, perhaps, I could place the restraint items there on the nightstand. Suzie was with me every step of the way, walking closely behind me, and I was scared. I hoped and prayed that she would calm down. That way, I wouldn't have to put to use that contraption ordered by the doctor for Suzie's and no less my safety.

When suddenly, Suzie let out a bloodcurdling scream, and of course I turned toward her. With an under-hand pitch swing of her arm, I was slapped on the side of my face with the water from the glass that I had placed on the nightstand. Then the glass fell to the floor. I kicked it under the bed, I guess so it could not be used as a weapon towards me anymore as water dipped from my face. I felt a sharp pain to my head as Suzie pulled at my long auburn hair, pulling me downward, and causing me to fall head first onto her double bed. Suzie came tumbling down and fell partially on me. We yelled at each other, screaming, mine were due to pain, as we tousled about. Then Suzie rolled on to her side landing by my side where she dug her hands deep in to my scalp, pulling at and twisting the strands of my hair around her fingers. And all the while snarling at me, enraged. I had yelled out in pain for her to stop, to let go of my hair, to behave! And as if someone turn off a switch, she stopped

. "Okay, Mum I'll be good!" She said and let go of my hair. But she couldn't remove her right entangled hand from the right side of the temple area of my head. So, I began to remove what hair I could from around her fingers, then simple pulled her hand out from my head. We both took a moment, for myself it was what seemed to be uncontrollable rubbing of my head and on occasion wiping some tears away. Suzie, on the other hand, smiled and simply caught her breath. I sighed a heavy sigh of relief and thanked God that I was now being referred to as Mum once more. It appeared to me that Suzie simply lived there at times behind the shadows of unresolved sorrow of her inner-child. Then I instructed her what to do and fastened the heavily Velcro laced straps of the vest in the back. And with one cooperative roll to the left, Suzie laid there on her back in the middle of her bed. I hurried off of the bed, although I'd stop to rub my head at time, I fasten the extended straps to the bed frame. Suzie was restrained to her bed only at her upper torso, I just couldn't totally strap my blue-eyed soul down. Her arms and legs had remained free. Trapped there in her sporadic emotions, it would have been better for those memories to have been erased from her mind. But no, they simply lied in wait for that oh so perfect time to torment their host... Suzie. An "Aha" moment for me, the inner-child's vicious cycle of misery. I felt the guilt of restraining Suzie, and for using her emotions that stemmed from her childhood tragedies to my advantage, to gain control. I sat there on the side of the bed, picked up the peach color warsh rag which was only damp to the touch. I brushed back her hair from those eyes of her, wiped her face, brushed some of the ashes from her hair, shoulders, blue dress and the bed. We both had cried a bit, as I felt my inner child emerging, wondering if in that state of mind, the children were then crying for each other. I swallowed hard and bit my inner cheek, that caused my lips to pucker, then my inner child left. So much scar tissue was there, so many bites over the years, I thought. Then I stood up, stood there, and placed a serious look on my face as if that would provide me strength. I carefully made my way about the bed wiping the ash off with the warsh rag down onto the navy-blue carpet. I cried a bit more and had asked God to forgive me. I watched as the ashes fell to the floor and by that time from myself as well. I continued to brush and brush off my body, the warsh rag lost its pretty peach color, so I placed it on the nearby dresser.

"I'm, a good girl, right Mum?" Suzie inquired of me. I had told her that was right, then stopped rubbing my head as hair fell and made its home on the floor too. I looked at he, my heart melted, and I wanted to remove the restraints, but instead told her she was an awesome girl. I shuddered, turned away to avoid eye contact and walked to the left side of the room. Looking at the opened bedroom door I wanted to flee. But I remained amongst the remains scattered there, where I could see the devastation of sorrow's woes as I stood there in the light; I remained there with what remained of Suzie, there in her childlike stage, and whatever state for myself. But there I stood with my back towards Suzie, but we were not alone. I cried, I thought it was pathetic of me, but nevertheless, I cried. I was not certain if it was because of Suzie's sorrow's woes, or for the awe of it all; or perhaps the pure mental anguish of it all that Suzie and I endured! I knew it not, and didn't care to try to understand anymore as I stopped crying. I had released my attempts of trying to understand - gave it up to God - he knows, and a relaxed calmness came over me. I felt my body relaxing as the darkness of the night carried on for Suzie and me.

"I heard you, you were crying! You're not the one tied down to the bed, lucky for you Bertha!" She stubbornly informed me as I turn around and looked at her. Her skin on her face was drawn inward to her forehead, wrinkled together lines, steel blue eyes that I could barely see, nose and mouth with their wrinkles all displayed in their various places, showed me their anger; I in turn told Suzie that I was Jamie, that Bertha was her mother's name.

"You're, a miserable bitch, Bertha, you blamed me for everything that went wrong in your life, even for Daddy leaving. I tried to be a good girl, but what did you do- you beat me!" she screamed in a disappointed irritated manner, in her adult voice. Hitting her balled up fist and arms on the bed while lifting her legs one at a time slamming them down onto the bed over and over again. Her actions like that of a two-year-old, temper tantrum in her emotional distress. Her screams were deafening to my ears, and no doubt could be heard outside and into the approaching night, but they would fall on deaf ears in our neighborhood. And this sadly, would continue on and off throughout the evening and into the night, but time for me and maybe for Suzie seemed to stand still.

There was a time when I could distract her from her fury, when I spoke of something of old, a song, a familiar place or talked about a character on a T.V. show. It was short lived, but somehow it always took her back to her memories of the 30's, the 50's. As she spoke it was like she was there, living in that very moment. She sang mostly sad songs that led her to what sounded like hysterical laugher and crying, followed by outbursts of screams. Time seemed to linger on-and-on, move on I prayed

. Yet, she told tales of love and love lost, I thought, yeah love lost all over the floor. But I mocked her not, it was merely a little levity for me to carry on then. After all, it was past midnight and she played out her pain and her pain played out on me. So many secrets were revealed, some I thought were better left unsaid. And as the night grew on, I couldn't imagine what it was she was going through there in the midst of her anguish. I was glad she would drink water from time to time. Suzie found herself exhausted at times, usually after a rage session of her display of uncontrolled anger and would not sleep. She kept a sharp eye on me watching me watch her.

However, it was in those times of Suzie's rest, what I called intermission time, where I attempted to retrieve as much of the ashes as I could. I used the dustpan and a broom, concentrating on the heavy ash area. Suzie laid there in silence glaring at me, keeping watch over my every move. There was no tiptoeing-around the room anymore, I simply worked to the right of the room, at the side window, and at the right side of the bed. Suzie would tell me to be careful at times, and would point out spots for me to work at, she was right. I placed the ashes that I was able to gather in to Raymond's urn, and placed the urn on top of the dresser adjacent to the mantle on the left in the sitting area of the room, in back of his picture. Then I closed my eyes, bowed my head and aloud said to God "thank you". I knew I would have to use the vacuum cleaner; the vacuum oh what an unwelcomed thought. I couldn't remember whatever happened to it; the mind so skillfully clever. Yet before the sun raised, I would do just that. So, I placed a new vacuum bag into the vacuum cleaner, and with a quick cleaning to the vacuum cleaner's rotating brush, I plugged it in. I had to take a deep breath and slowly let it out as I turned the vacuum cleaner on. The vacuum's sound aided me, with its hum-hum sound that would drown out the sound of Suzie's words, but I could still see her eyes, so I stopped looking at her, a tragic event for the two of us no doubt. I simply concentrated on my work pausing only to pick up my hair, pushing it down into my right blue jean back pocket. I kept my heard down with only glances at Suzie at times, but I felt her eyes on me. Unfortunately, the vacuum's sound could not mask the sound of the rapid succession of cracking noise of pulverized bones that were being sucked up! I felt depleted and had asked God to forgive me, then continued on. I then removed the vacuum bag, there was quite a good amount, and emptied the contents into the other urn placing the urn on the same dresser and behind his picture. I looked up and said out loud "forgive us Lord" pausing for a moment, then said "thank you". Then walking over to the opposite side of the room adjacent to the door, I placed the bag on the dresser beside the warsh rag.

I felt utterly spent and it seemed like I felt the heaviness of the events on my shoulders as the wee hours of the night continued on. Suzie pleaded for help and of course I didn't know why.

"Oh, help me please, I'll be a good girl Mum!" Suzie sadly whispered but in her normal speaking voice. This of course drew me into walking over to her and I sat on the bed. There appeared to be nothing physically wrong with her, I checked the back of the vest, placing my hand between the mattress and Suzie's back and felt the Velcro it was still in place. I asked her if she wanted it off, yet she didn't respond. Nor at any time did she ask to be released, she only continued on and on asking for help.

"Please, help me. I'll be a good girl, Mum", Suzie pleaded humbly. "Please help me, I'll be a good girl."

Time moved on with no end to her repeating the same pleas. Oh, how I wanted her misery to end, to help her. I thought her mad, but what more could I have done. I gave her water but she would not drink. I offered her tea, something to eat, but she would not answer. I tried holding her hand, but she withdrew it from me. I tried to care for my blue-eyed soul, but nothing would do. I played the part of Mom attempting to sooth her, but that only made her frantic and she began to yell out her plea. So, I removed myself from the side of her bed, and found myself pacing the floor. I guessed she wanted to be freed from her suffering. Wouldn't we all, of course, yet I could not soothe her in any way, nor find a way to help her. I could deal with the violent outbursts, but Suzie trapped in what seemed like a consuming torment, this long suffering of hers, had to end! I could bear it no more as I sunk into what seemed like despair. I told myself to breathe, and did so, then reminded myself that God was with us.

"Please, help me. I'll be a good girl Mum!" Suzie said. "Please help me, I'll be a good girl, Mom," with tears that fell from her soulful eyes. I had nothing more to offer of myself. Having heard her cries in that moment, I wondered why God didn't use a better person then me to help Suzie. Then I thought, there were none better, we're all sinners, we all fell short of God's glory. And in my pacing about the room, I'd found myself at the side of Suzie's bed. Dropping down to the floor on my knees, reaching up for Suzie's right hand, our eyes met and she extended her hand to me, yet, all the while continuing in her pleas. Then I took her hand in my left hand and held it. Her hand felt so fragile and I held on gently. My body quivered inside, but I remained on my knees, then clearing my throat, resting on my faith in that of the truth of the Lord, I began to pray:

"Our Father, who art in heaven, hallowed
Be thy Name, thy Kingdom come, thy will be done, on
Earth as it is in heaven,
Give us this day our daily bread.
And forgive us our trespasses as we forgive those who trespass against us
And lead us not into temptation, but
Deliver us from evil. For thine is the Kingdom, and
the power, and the glory, forever and ever. Amen"

The Lord's Prayer resonated in Suzie's bed room, and I held onto Suzie's hand. She held onto mine and squeezed it at times. I continued on and on; verse after verse, repeating the Lord's Prayer. Suzie chimed in with a cracked shaking voice, tears rapidly fell from her blue eyes. Breaking her out of her pleading for help stage, at times our voices prayed in unison as we wept.

I removed the restraints and attempted to assist Suzie in siting up, but she hugged me instead, then laid back down with a pleasant look on her face. The sun rose and seemed to fill the room with light. Suzie's torment was over!

Oh, the power of prayer, it was not a faded age of faith, no only one truth. There in that place a miracle; that quieted Suzie's suffering. I rejoiced in his holy name, Hallelujah! And felt joy in the very core of me, for I knew random acts of kindness were not random at all. Thanking God for his show of kindness to Suzie ...me too. Suzie was tormented no more, appearing peaceful and with a sparkle in those eyes of hers, and wearing a smile on her face. Acts of kindness are deliberate, profound, purposeful acts, made out of love.

"I feel much better, thanks to God!" Suzie proclaimed

I smile and had said, "Tea"?

"Yes, please!" she cheerfully replied.

I wanted to question Suzie as to what she thought happened with her, but somehow, I knew she wouldn't be able to tell me. So, I made my exit from Suzie's room stopping on the stairs midway down, looked up into Suzie's bed room, she laid on her side facing the opened door remaining calm, looking content. I continued my descent down those steps giving thanks and praise to our Lord, downward to fetch the morning tea.

2003

Everyday life moved on, as it does, and as the months turned into years Mom moved on too. Mom found herself moving away from all that was familiar to her, and had entered a Skilled Nursing home. Mom came from the chaos of the *Silent Generation* era. She lived through the Great Depression and World War II's effects on her life. Life was a struggle for Mom from the start with the lack of value placed on the children who grew up in that era. I guessed that was part of the reason why Mom and I had a detached relationship. Mom was a survivor then, and I hoped she would be able to survivor the short stay in the Skilled Nursing home, or that they survived her. As I brought a small suitcase of clothing out to my car to take to the home, I lingered about in the yard. After closing the car's trunk, I zipped my heavy jacket up and leaned on the car and found myself staring into the yard, remembering. My mind went to a time spent with Mom one sunny day in July.

I recalled the warmth of the day and the sweet sounds of summer; I was twelve then and we sat there in the yard on the glider under the shade of big oak tree. That glider had been painted so often that the burnt orange under coat bled through the yellow and white top coats of paint. Mom had her feet soaking in a pink rectangular hospital warsh basin; her flowered dress pulled up to her thighs and tucked in between her upper inner thighs of her beautiful shapely legs. She held the green garden hose in her right hand resting the hose nozzles on her closed thighs. The water from the hose then cascaded down from the thighs, legs and went into the basin below. I enjoyed the giggles and oohs that Mom made reacting to the cold water. I heard the kids up the street playing and the birds, all good sounds, but the "giggles and oohs" was summer to me. The water went into the warsh basin below and over flowed splashing onto the red brick paved ground of the yard. Yet, I had been playing a game in the water with my feet as I sat beside Mom there to the left of her. I tried to stop the water with my feet before it was able to reach the red ground. I put both feet together kept my toes together moving them back and forth before the water made its escape, splashing down to be carried off though the different lines between the bricks, like a superhighway. Sometimes I'd stomp down to change its direction once it got pass my feet. The cool water had been a welcome treat on a rather warm day as we had sat there together enjoying it waiting for Dad.

Mom had grown rather annoyed about how long it was taking Dad to arrive home, so she turned to me, looked me in the eyes, and as sweet as could be had asked if I wanted to hear a story. I excitingly had answered her yes and my pins and needles were activated! Mom had told me that before I was born, she and Dad had been separated. She was on her way of being over him until that evening in July.

"I, looked out my bedroom window and there he was, your Dad! He had sat in his car across the street from the house looking up at my bedroom window, at me. I yelled down to him, told him to leave, but he told me never. I grinned a little and against my better judgement went downstairs, and let him back into my life, and in my bed. Then you came along, I never wanted you, Jamie, never!" Mom proclaimed with a sarcastic tone. She laughed! Oh, how she was laughing, a hearty laugh right in my face! So, I laughed too, although mine was one to mask my pain, then simply laughing along with her since hers was such a joyful one; you know laughter is contagious. But I had stopped way before Mom did, I felt deeply saddened, it wasn't that contagious! I felt like I was about to cry, but instead I thought, cue the sad music and hung my head low, wrung my hands together and was watched the water as it over flowed from the basin.

I was a useful tool to Mom and at least I knew why. To put it simply, I caught hell; all I knew was that words were spoken, things were done, something set Mom off and I was there. I would be hit, slapped, pushed down- told to get up only to be knocked back down. And I had to get up quick or...I'll leave it alone, along with the verbal display of her anger to your imagination. I could recall praying for Mom to get a true friend, someone she could talk to. I always thought maybe a friend could have helped, what could it have hurt or, yeah, me.

Dad knew Mom was jealous of me, he had said concerning our relationship because she didn't have a Father/Daughter relationship of her own. Dad taught me at an early age how to stay out of Mom's hair, whatever that meant! I didn't listen to his instructions well enough, but eventually I got it. I was able to avoid trouble sometimes, yet at times she caught on and said I was placating her, whatever that meant. She said that I should have stopped listening to my Dad about treating her a certain way... that spelled a special kind of trouble for me.

"I need money, the kids need shoes. Have you seen their shoes, Gus?" Mom had asked of Dad.

I looked down at my shoes; they seemed fine to me; Mom always asked for money it seemed. Dad stood there in the kitchen by his chair, he had not sat down yet.

"Here this should do it," Dad angrily replied in his deep strong voice, "I don't have any more money!"

Reaching in his right back pants pocket of his navy-blue work pants he took out his wallet, then opened it. I stood by him watching every move as he took money out folding it, then handed it to me.

“Here, Jamie, give this to your Mum,” He indicated in a loving manner, smiled at me and gave me a hug; then turned walking out the kitchen door. It seemed like Dad was always leaving! I gave Mom the money as she passed by me following behind Dad. She quickly looked it over, then tucked it in that safe place between her bra and her right breast. I, of course, followed slowly behind them both.

“Oh, you’re leaving Gus?” Mom inquired of him in an angry tone of voice. While Dad kept walking, I ran past Mom and caught up to him. Mom then stopped and walked back to the kitchen door, standing in between the door and the screen door holding it open with her right hand and forearm leaning out a bit. She glared at Dad, watching our every move as we stood together beside his black four-door shiny car. I hugged him, asking him to stay, but he shook his head. I then asked for some money to roller skate.

“Not, you too, Jamie?” Dad said.

Dad winked his right eye; “like I told your Mom, I don’t have any more money.”

the money would be. That was a lot of money for a nine-year-old at that time, but I was Daddy’s little girl. One more kiss for a thank you and a goodbye and I happily skipped off to go back into the house.

“Jamie!” he yelled.

I turned quick and had waited.

"Tell Mum I'll be back in a bit," he said cheerfully and I hurried into the house to that. I knew Dad's "a bit" meant hours later. But he always said that, I hoped for Mom's sake it wasn't too long. I had told Mom what Dad said, but she didn't say anything to me as she stood at the stove, her back to me. She had been cooking my favorite, spaghetti. I smelled it from outside, so good.

"I, don't like it, Jamie, you telling me," she indicated in a rather calm voice, "You're always chasing him away."

I knew not to say anything, but boy-oh-boy I wanted to. Instead, I shook my head, sticking out my tongue while I made a smarty-pants face at her! I knew I wasn't the one that chased Dad away! Yet, Mom always said she had eyes in the back of her head, turning around she caught me in the very act. I was shocked, there was no surprise look on her face and she turned back to the stove and turned off the fire from under the sauce pot and no words were spoken, from Mom that was. I on the other hand, I was doing enough talking for the both of us. I tried to explain my way out of things. I covered my mouth, then coughed and explained to Mom that I had just been coughing, an early summer cold, I said, then coughed some

and placed it by her chair at her kitchen table. I remember that it looked like I had been dancing around the kitchen, trying desperately to get her attention and went far enough to bribe her with the five bucks. She then opened up the middle junk drawer and took out the brown extension cord. I could plead no more to Mom, my words fell on deaf ears. So, I asked God to help me as Mom spoke, but I think God must have been busy helping others out that late day.

"Come, here, Jamie!" Mom demanded.

She sat on her chair with that brown extension cord in her right hand.

It was the most excruciating special beating of them all. I had breathed a heavy sigh, then swallowed hard. I slowly walked to Mom, looking down, I had cut off blue jean shorts on and a pink T- shirt. She sat waiting there for me with a peeved look upon her face; I took a deep breath in, slowly letting it out and I was there. I looked Mom in her eyes and told her I was ready! I'm not sure what came over me but I had courage! Mom dipped the cord in the red bucket of water, and I had noticed something I never did before. I heard the drips of the water that fell from the cord when she pulled it from the bucket. I watched curiously, It was the most excruciating special beating of them all. I had breathed a heavy sigh, then swallowed hard. I slowly walked to Mom, looking down, I had cut off blue jean shorts on and a pink T- shirt. She sat waiting there for me with a peeved look upon her face; I took a deep breath in, slowly letting it out and I was there. I looked Mom in her eyes and told her I was ready! I'm not sure what came over me but I had courage! Mom dipped the cord in the red bucket of water, and I had noticed something I never did before. I heard the drips of the water that fell from the cord when she pulled it from the bucket. I watched curiously, but somewhat frightened; watched the water slide down the cord forming two drips, then plink-plink, fell into the red bucket of water. I thought those were my tears and there they were going to be. I watched the cord as it was set in motion, listening to the swish sound it made, breathing slowly but bracing myself for the hit, but then felt my body relax. This was new, I thought as the whip sound of the cord and the letter "J" of my name was being said. That horrible cord had made its contact as Mom had swung it like a whip, and it landed on my upper right thigh. Pain, yes, but not so much! I continued to breathe slowly; I didn't scream. Mom had such a puzzled look on her face, which gave me strength. I found myself repeating the word "concentrate", so I did. And I watched as Mom stood up and said the letter "A" in my name. Watching intensely as she made the dip into the red bucket, dangling the cord over it as the water made its way down forming five drips then. I said there are my tears; plink-plink-plink-plink-plink! The swish, the snap and the hit! I pulled my lips in and pressed down hard, my big brown eyes widened and tears formed in my eyes, but none fell as I continued to slowly breathe. No screams, only a movement of my body as it took the hit. I didn't dance around the room crying and pleading. No! I simply stood there waiting, repeating the word "concentrate". I was pushed to the kitchen floor and quickly, but painfully, got up and whimpered slightly, then stood there like a little Soldier. Mom's eyes grew wide with surprise- with shock! I guessed I didn't amuse her anymore.

"Give me that money you got from your Dad and go to your room, little bitch!" Mom hollered.

I gave her the five bucks, then told her thank you.

"Go!" She demanded.

And I went as fast as I could, leaving the kitchen behind me, passing through the hall, the dining room, the front hall and then up the steps. It was there, on the steps, I noticed that there was blood on my right thigh, but I didn't care. I made my way to my room there in the attic. I knew it was God that helped me. He didn't stop the beating, yet, my name wasn't spelled out either, He stayed with me; He gave me strength, He was there!

It seemed like I caused a lot of arguments between Mom and Dad back then. I guess I wasn't so clever after all. Dad had returned home from his "in-a-bit" time out. And I had to endure his lecture, right after their argument, that was. I've got to admit, Mom's beating was a lot faster than Dad's hour-long lecture, and I could get on with the rest of my day. I felt bad, though, for Dad. All he wanted was to rest from his long time on the road. I felt sorry for Mom. I should not have treated Mom that way, nor made faces behind her back. There's something in the Bible about being good to parents, and I was wrong. It didn't matter if I was nine years old, I felt sorry for me too.

I rubbed my scar on my upper right thigh while I got into the car and put the heat on the low setting to warm me form the chilly sunny March day. Time went by quickly and the chilly weather seemed so fitting for my reflections. I sat there in the car enjoying the warmth and thought how grateful I was to be a morning person. Reflecting on the Lord, I gave Him thanks and praised the Lord for the day, and what it would bring. I prayed that I could understand my sorrow, or at least part of it so I could let it go. Having heard my request, I thought it best to look to Godly sorrow which leads to salvation than worldly sorrow that produces death. I loved Mom, and I prayed for her too. I prayed for a speedy recovery, to a peaceful return home; yet, in that recovery process that she would get to know You better, amen. Then turning on the music, I drove away not bothering to use my rearview mirror. I was glad that the windshield was much bigger. I was on my way to the Nursing home.

The ride was somewhat of a distance from that old house, and even further from my house. But I had arrived, turning left into the Nursing Home's parking lot. There were piles of snow piled high in various side spots of the lot. I left the warmth of my car, pulling my jacket sides together, and held them there as I made my way to the back of the car to get the suitcase out. Clutching my jacket, while I used the suitcase as a shield against the then cold breeze touching my face and ran to the building's door.

I was welcomed into the building to a grilling heat at the main hall and immediately removed my jacket. I continued on in that grilling heat down the corridors, the temperature seemed to increase and was then accompanied by a strong chemical disinfectant with a splash of urine and medicinal smells. That smell far exceeded any stink from any thrift store. I made my way to the D-wing, there was a nurse's station right outside to the left of room 446, Mom's room, and so there was no need to stop there to inquire of the "where about" for the room.

I was approached by the Social Worker just as I was about to open the door to room 446. She was more than happy to inform me that Mom and my relationship was dysfunctional. I told her, yes, that I was well aware of our dysfunctional relationship. I told her how we as humans formed our core relationships in our childhood. I added how we would relate to our self's and to others based on that foundation. I told her that I understood, but we were not void of love and compassion. We were broken, but weren't we all. I wasn't relying on my dysfunctional foundation, but on God's foundation. And as her mouth dropped opened, I smiled politely nodding my head and bid her a good day, then opened the door. I didn't bother to tell her that I was a Christian and a

Social Worker too. I'd hoped my actions were enough. Good, bad or indifferent, I loved my Mom.

I entered the room and my ears were treated to a delightful sound. I heard Mom's sweet voice as she sang along with the radio. An instant smile appeared on my face as I stood there, then closed my eyes and just listened. It was a little bit trembling sounding, yet soulful, soothing to me. She sang in what I thought to be a breathy sounding voice, or something like that. Whatever it was, for a moment I was lost in the sound of Mom's voice, it was wonderful to me. Mom sat there on a dark gray easy chair close to the wall with no window, I thought it odd. I made a slight coughing sound to gain her attention as not to startle her. She raised her head, her gray with streaks of red hair was her crown.

"Oh, hello there," Mom said in a cheerful manner, yet needing to take a breath. I placed the suitcase down on the vinyl wooden looking floor. I clapped yelling encore – encore! We both laughed, but my laughter quickly decreased then stopped; it always did. Oh, but when she did laugh, it was a hearty one from the soul I thought. I wanted to hear more singing but the oldies station that had been playing went into a block of advertisements. And with suitcase in hand; I went farther into the room, turning down the volume on the radio that was on the nightstand by the phone next to Mom's hospital bed.

"How's, the weather out there," She inquired.

Walking over to her I extended my hand to her. Sitting down in the brown and beige striped wingback chair beside her I told her to feel for herself. I then placed the case on the floor beside my chair and the dresser.

"Oh, it's so cold!" She said pulling her right hand back for a moment, then placing both of her hands on my left hand in attempted to warm my hand with what little warmth she had of her own.

A gentle smile rose upon my face.

I had replied telling her that it was sunny and there was a coolness to the day, but when the wind blow across the piles of snow in the lot it could be chill. But it was beautiful, the crisp cool air was refreshing.

"Yes, it would be nice to have a window," she sighed as we held hands then.

"My hands look so old! Look at the long bony fingers, look the girl painted my nails light pink – not the color that I like," she said.

The skin of her hands resembled that of a tissue that had been balled up then opened and laid flat displaying the passing of time. And yet they were so soft. I held them, looked at them, then said the word "beautiful", and she smile. We had both agreed that my hands looked like hers when I was a kid. Then I sighed, because I was then forty, forty years old and felt it too in that heat that made me sweaty, and the smells I had to endure at the home. Yet, I maintained my figure, but of course, I wasn't twenty anymore. I was quite youthful looking, though, being mistaken for being in my thirties. I had inherited the youthful gene from Dad, people would say. However, I wiped my brow and carried on displaying the clothing from the suitcase for Mom, then folding them and placing them in the nearby dresser's third drawer. The two top drawers were filled, one with toiletry items and the other with a bed pan on one side and to the other side towels and warsh rags. When Mom had seen the white sweater, she wanted me to help her put it on. I did so, but the sight of her with it on had made me feel even hotter and I had better cool down or I would add to the smells. So, I relied on my imagination to help keep me cool, thought of the piles of snow as my eyes fell on the wall of the room. It was a great canvas for my imagination to express itself, and I was soon cool. In a reclining position, Mom had fallen asleep, her head and neck were in a good position, so I wasn't concerned, and I let her sleep. I'd hoped that the call alerts wouldn't wake her too soon. I wondered why the walls were bare and of such a dull state, off-white in color. Oh, there was a sign on the door in the corner of the room that read "handicap accessible", which made me laugh at its meaning. Then I looked over at Mom, still asleep. The word Handicap and the word Accessible together – barrier-- no-barrier, made no sense. I thought of it as décor for the room. Behind the door, however, was a well-equipped bathroom to accommodate those with a handicap. Although, I wondered, if room 446 was a result of those with failing eyesight; Mom had tunnel-vision. I thought the room should be the opposite; eye-catching in color, and at least a room with a view for patients with failing eye sight, or any patient for that matter. It was a good thing that I had brought Mom's teddy bear and the picture of her and her sibling that she loved. I hoped they would help her with her stay. I got up from the chair placing the picture on top of the small dresser directly across from her bed. I could reach the dresser from a seated position, but wanted it to be centered. Mind you, it was a small room and I was quite sure she would be able to see it when in bed. I couldn't wait for her to see it.

Mom had woken and wanted to be in the bed. I started to assist her when two aides entered and informed me that they would take it from there. It was time for Mom to be refreshed before lunch, so I was sent out of the room.

Break time, out to the lounge area I went. I was not alone; several people had been kicked out of their loved one's room so patients could use the facilities and be refreshed. I kept my head down until a man said hello, and we talked. We talked about anything, but nothing concerning where we were, for whom, or why. It had been a pleasant conversation that took us past the lunch hour before we noticed the time. Then we said our goodbyes returning to our love ones.

Mom was indeed refreshed, her hair had been brushed she had a nightgown on and smelled like lavender, a welcome smell, and she was where she wanted to be; in bed. However, she seemed somewhat frail as the wrinkled lines and lose skin of her right arm shook as her hand trembled when she reached over her body attempting to turn off the radio. Her breath was labored and her nostrils flared. She had widened her eyes, I assumed in the attempt to see better, or was it due to the strain. The empty skin of her cheeks and neck hung over to the left side as she reached even farther. Her mostly gray hair fell down from its brushed back position covering most of her widen blue eyes. This caused her to tumble forward clumsily knocking the telephone onto its side. I picked up and put the phone back in place, then turned off the radio. She moved on to her back resting and catching her breath. I gave Mom a drink of water from a cup through a straw.

I thanked the aide, who took the cup from my hand replacing it with a freshly poured water in a Styrofoam cup, then placed the pitcher of water on the food tray to the right side of the bed.

"Looks like she needed a drink! I'm Kim, are you alright Mrs. Suzie?" Kim asked my Mom. As my Mom was still drinking, Mom nodded in response. Walking to the tray, I placed the cup by the pitcher then went and stood at the foot of the bed. Kim adjusted Mom's body, cradling Mom's head and neck as she fluffed up the pillow, then returned her head to it on the bed. Kim then located the cord to the call button and placed it in Mom's hand. Then extending my Mom's arm down to her side, Kim took the call button out of her hand and patted on the bed.

"Mrs. Suzie, can you pick up the call button for me?" Kim asked.

Mom patted the bed to locate it then picked it up.

"That's good, Mrs. Suzie. Feel the button, just push it if you need anything. I'm Kim, I'll be your aide till midnight," She informed.

Mom pushed the button.

"That's good, we know it works. Did you need anything else Mrs. Suzie?" she inquired.

"Oh," Mom said, "no," in a rather weak voice I was not used to hearing. Kim turned away from the bed to leave the room then paused turning back around and gave me a strange look, then left the room. Peculiar, I wondered, what that was all about, but soon dismissed it. Looking at Mom, my blue-eyed soul as she was in a relaxed state, she smiled. The wrinkles around her lips but all disappeared as the ones at her eyes increased. I smiled too because I could see her there, the Beauty that she became and was. I had seen them both there. Oh, my blue-eyed soul, I thanked God for her. And we talked low and slow sometimes in a sweet whisper like the distant sound of a cardinal – a distant whisper of a visitor from heaven. It was Sunday, March 9, 2003, 5:46 p.m. on that day of Suzie's weakened state.

It was dinner time, the tray was placed on the food tray, the pitcher of water removed and put onto the dresser almost knocking the picture to the floor; and Suzie – Mom - noticed it there. Her eyes widened, followed by a sound of an "oh". Then the picture was put back in place by Kim. I helped by opening that which needed to be opened on the food tray, preparing the tea, while Kim worked on Suzie putting her in an upright position and then she left room 446. I placed the food tray in front of her, we gave thanks, and with an "Amen" Suzie tried to feed herself even though her hand was shaky. She had experienced difficulties with eye-hand coordination too, so her attempt was just that. It was my pleasure to feed her, although she ate very little of the mash potatoes and meat loaf, but drank all her tea. Kim came in to chart the food intake information by simply looking at the plate and then adjusted the bed to Suzie's liking and left without a strange look.

Suzie was falling in and out of sleep so I took that time to center the picture. I got the teddy bear out and placed in the bed. Our time together was winding down; Kim was back in the room with the night medication and dismissed me to the lounge area once again for the night hygiene tasks for Suzie to take place. She informed me that once I saw the room door partially open, I could return. And I was back in the room at 7 o'clock. She was nice and clean and a delightful aroma filled the room once again.

She was wearing a hospital grown and appeared to be drained of energy, just like a new born baby sleeps after being bathed. So, I didn't what to prolong her sleep, I told her that she looked beautiful, asking what I could bring her for tomorrow.

In a tiny fragile voice Suzie answered me, "something sweet, get home to your family," and with an Eskimo kiss, a kiss on the lips, a good night-God bless and a see you later, our visit came to an end. At the nurse's station I inquired of Kim's whereabouts, she was completing her rounds. I would have to address the look at a later time. And I made my way through the building anticipating the cool crisp fresh air. Then, I was there inhaling it – a celebration to my nose.

The ride home was, of course, faster. I could usually be home in about 15 minutes. I was happy Suzie and I had developed a different type of relationship that took place partly when I moved out of my parent's house. It seemed to have come into full bloom a while after Dad was called home. I noticed at times in the quietness of silent memories of Dad, he nudged me; reminding me of the place he used to be. I knew for me the world was a bit quieter, a little colder – void of his warmth and missing the presence of his joy. Dad was Dad; I never referred to my Dad as Father, unless you want to count the time Suzie and I baked him a Father's Day cake. But even then, I had spelled "Further" on the cake – a seven-year-old Freudian slip. Because as far back as I could remember, I sought after my Heavenly Father. Throughout my life I've loved him in various ways, based on my development/ a relationship in my thoughts, words, acts and deeds. He's a part of me, and was always there even in the times when I didn't want him to be. I'd stray away- away from the true purpose. And my Lord called me back to where I belonged, time and time again. I would keep him in my everyday life, asking for guidance and more. Yet, I had to do my part, and that required trusting in God, surrendering my control- such a scary thing. But I had known my life was not my own. Could I then The ride home was, of course, faster. I could usually be home in about 15 minutes. I was happy Suzie and I had developed a different type of relationship that took place partly when I moved out of my parent's house. It seemed to have come into full bloom a while after Dad was called home. I noticed at times in the quietness of silent memories of Dad, he nudged me; reminding me of the place he used to be. I knew for me the world was a bit quieter, a little colder – void of his warmth and missing the presence of his joy. Dad was Dad; I never referred to my Dad as Father, unless you want to count the time Suzie and I baked him a Father's Day cake. But even then, I had spelled "Further" on the cake – a seven-year-old Freudian slip. Because as far back as I could remember, I sought after my Heavenly Father. Throughout my life I've loved him in various ways, based on my development/ a relationship in my thoughts, words, acts and deeds. He's a part of me, and was always there even in the times when I didn't want him to be. I'd stray away- away from the true purpose. And my Lord called me back to where I belonged, time and time again. I would keep him in my everyday life, asking for guidance and more. Yet, I had to do my part, and that required trusting in God, surrendering my control- such a scary thing. But I had known my life was not my own. Could I then The ride home was, of course, faster. I could usually be home in about 15 minutes. I was happy Suzie and I had developed a different type of relationship that took place partly when I moved out of my parent's house. It seemed to have come into full bloom a while after Dad was called home. I noticed at times in the quietness of silent memories of Dad, he nudged me; reminding me of the place he used to be. I knew for me the world was a bit quieter, a little colder – void of his warmth and missing the presence of his joy. Dad was Dad; I never referred to my Dad as Father, unless you want to count the time Suzie and I baked him a Father's Day cake. But even then, I had spelled "Further" on the cake – a seven-year-old Freudian slip. Because as far back as I could remember, I sought after my Heavenly Father. Throughout my life I've loved him in various ways, based on my development/ a relationship in my thoughts, words, acts and deeds. He's a part of me, and was always there even in the times when I didn't want him to be. I'd stray away- away from the true purpose. And my Lord called me back to where I belonged, time and time again. I would keep him in my everyday life, asking for guidance and more. Yet, I had to do my part, and that required trusting in God, surrendering my control- such a scary thing. But I had known my life was not my own. Could I then

present myself before God, report card in hand to prove I've been a good person – here - look at my good grades; No! On the contrary, I was not perfect nor would I ever be. I could not earn his love. For I knew our relationship was possible by Jesus' Salvation and of God's unmerited Grace. There was nothing that I had done or could do. I am nothing without God, best that I remained in His love. And it was that love which allowed me to care for my blue-eyed soul after Dad passed away; Suzie and I were together for two years.

All this I thought, as I found myself parked and sat in my car in front of the old house, not remembering the drive there. The house was empty then, and twenty- five years of my life was there, how I'd wished it would be torn down. When suddenly – Oh what's this there in the living room, I heard laughter, and 1- 2- 3 beat as if it was music. Yes, I remembered how we use to dance the waltz there; in the living room. The beautiful ornate chandelier casting its light about the room as Suzie and I would dance. Yes, I remembered as a smile came upon my face then tears followed. It seemed like we were floating around as the years had gone by with our dance, dancing only to Suzie's count, I had forgotten how we loved to dance. Oh, what's this, I so conceived pleasant scenes of Mother and Daughter, they came flooding into my mind's eye. There in Suzie's room warmly snuggled back-to-back under one of her homemade quilts, I felt a heartfelt warmth as I listened to her as she sang old county songs.

Then there in various rooms flashed visions of her brushing my hair, one hundred strokes in all, all with loving care it had seemed. Yes, there was affection for me from Suzie, not in a hug or a kiss of a hello or goodbye, nor when I fell down skinning my knee. But it was in our rhythm of our dance we had together, our warmth created from our being back-to-back on those cold winter's night. It was with the sweetest sad songs I ever heard that she sung dancing in my ears. It was with the touch of Suzie's hand on my head as she gently stocked the hair on my head. The brush stroke found its way down to the ends of my thick long auburn hair. How she held my hair just so, so I could not feel any tugs when she happens upon a tangle in my hair, and with every passing stroke. Oh, the warmth of her hand, Dear Lord, I could feel it. Was this a mystery then unfolding, I thought? All this beauty I saw amongst the fragmented pieces. I had to put the pieces together, I had seen the beauty that was within her. Miseries, did I wade in them as to wade in muddy waters of self- pity, for so many years my only focus just that? I hoped not! I was sure that passed sorrow's woe for the most part came up tugging at me, at my heart, at myself-esteem at times, and at times the very cord of me - breaking my spirit down. No, I called upon them solemnly, in times when my efforts failed me. I had no answer for the purpose of this sweet bitter experience; I knew God did, yet it was quite difficult to leave it at that. I dried my eyes, put some music on, then drove away one last look in the rearview mirror watching as the distance between me and that old Victorian house grew and headed for home.

It was 3 o' clock on Monday, and I had felt a sense of urgency to get to Suzie. Of course, the drive seemed longer then but you know, that's always the case when you're in a hurry. I was filled with anticipation. Even though the drive was not far from my work place, I had to contend with crazy drivers. All but me, since I made the best moves, I thought possible through traffic. Honking the car horn for the drivers ahead of me to move at the very second the light had turned green, because I had waited long enough. I had the music on, one of my five friends I had that touched my soul. I played it in an attempt to clear my thoughts. However, it didn't touch anything that day, maybe a nerve. Thank God I was almost there, about a block or so away from the red light then a right at the intersection into the lot and I was there. But before I got out of the car, I gave thanks and said: "Thank you Lord for the day, thank you for the way; thank you for our lives, and loving us, Amen."

I made my way inside, stopping in the main lobby at the pop machine and got a cold orange pop. As I reached the fourth floor passing the nurse's station, one of the nurses told me to take a seat in the lounge. I thought, and put it with silly thoughts, help me not be so serious regarding serious situations.

" I will let the doctor know that you're here." she said.

So, I took my imaginary chair and sat down in the lobby and reflected on the past, not to have my mind jumping to wild conclusions. I had thought about the time Suzie and I were the only two, besides God, in that big old house of ours. She had a sense of urgency about her as if she had a premonition that Dementia was about to rise its ugly head in her life. So, we talked, or should I say, she did a great deal of it. Yet the more we talked, the closer we became, slowly forming a new relationship. It must have been a great deal of soul searching for Suzie to speak of the contempt she had held for me when I was child, I suppose. Her being a stern proud woman, this spoke volumes about her character and was a lesson for me then. She had humbled herself to the point of tears before she even spoke a word. It wasn't guilt-ridden, I had seen that look on her face before; this look was definitely different. And for some reason, I got up from the bench and sat in Dad's old chair directly across from Suzie to put some distance between the two of us. I wasn't sure what was coming next. I had never seen that look before, so I braced myself.

"I love you, Jamie, but I couldn't love you when you were a kid. I didn't want you because I knew Gus would love you more than me. He was right! Oh, Jamie how I envied your relationship you had with your Dad- I wanted that too! And over the years you became like a Mother that I never had, and I let you. I hated the fact that I needed you, and look where we are today, here, sitting in this kitchen together the two of us! God gave you broad shoulders, Jamie. You carried a great deal of my life's load on them, and so much more. He made you strong, Jamie, He made you strong!" Suzie sincerely informed me.

I felt my eyes widen and my heart seemed to be in my throat. And before I had the chance to look up at her, she was out of her chair quickly walking towards me. She bent over stooping down to me, looked me in the eyes with her steel blue eyes, and gentle said that she loved me. Then Suzie had asked for my forgiveness; yet, there was nothing to forgive (joy-an internal feeling that disregards circumstances). Oh, Mom (Suzie), but how the child in me melted and my face changed in seconds from shock to contentment. I felt Suzie's words had made their way down to my very soul! Then in a standing position, I held Suzie so endearingly. I felt the warmth of our bodies, our breathing and I felt as if the past years rushed by with various stages of our ages present within the sweetness of our embrace. And I was "within" and "of" that moment; that was the best feeling (learned behaviors that are usually in hibernation until triggered by an external event) I ever had between the two of us. Then she had to tell me to let go. I did as she told me, still I remained in those feelings taking deep breaths as if to take it all in, locking it away. I giggled like a child (happy, happiness was the state of my mind based on circumstances). It was a lot of unusual emotions (event – driven) for me to process that day. It happened that day; I didn't know joy till then. I had seen a flashback of myself on my bike, my arms spread as my wings. How I tried to be free, to catch freedom within the glide not really quite sure of what it was I desperately trying to break free of, or why I was born, and what did God want me to do? The flashback faded away, but I remembered when I had come down from that natural high, I couldn't recall if Mom every told me she loved me when I was a kid. And you know what, it didn't matter anymore. I was released! I had no more use for licking old wounds, as far as it came to wondering if Mom my blue-eyed soul loved me. God found me, and my freedom from Mom was gained, and so much more.

"God is everywhere, Jamie, keep him in your everyday life!" Suzie professed and I wept as she held me.

"Jamie, Jamie, you can go in, the doctor is done," the nurse said.

Walking into Suzie's room, I was greeted by her doctor in his dingy white coat and the nutritionist who looked very tired. They had both turned away from Suzie and faced me, their back to her. The doc placed his stethoscope around his neck, its working parts rested on both sides of his chest, their bodies blocking my view of Suzie. I said hello, looking beyond them and they, both answered separating one to the other. There were only a few steps for me to take, and I made it to her bedside. Yet I found I had placed my feet on the floor in a careful manner as if I had walked on unstable ground. I then bent in with a kiss on the mouth and a "hey Mom", which yielded no responses other than the fluttering of her eyes. I looked quite puzzled with concern as I stood in the up- right position, walking over to the two of them, and stood amongst them after taking three steps back and facing Suzie to hear what they had to say.

"Hello again, Jamie it's time to spend quality time with your mom and let the family know to visit soon," the doctor informed.

"Your Mom can eat and drink whatever she wants," the nutritionist cheerfully informed. I'll continue to monitor her intake, and her ability to chew and swallow over the course of her declining health."

My puzzled look was no more than concern that my Suzie had possibly heard this news in such a way and I inquired as such. Oh, you should have seen the looks on their faces, it was like they required medical attention, appearing as if the blood had drained from their faces. Then they looked at one another with a perplexed look upon their faces, looking at my Suzie and walking closer to her, they called out her name and informing her of, her declining health in great details. I had to admit I couldn't hear a word they said other than stage, then I chinned in. I asked if she had heard what was said.

"Yes, I'm tired, not dead," Suzie replied in a weak, shaky, but rather feisty voice; and I had to smile, I couldn't stop it. I thought; "that's my blue-eyed soul". With that said, they made their way out of the room with not another word to offer her- like words, any questions or concerns. Nevertheless, I was glad for their departure and got my kiss. I picked up a new straw, popped the pop open and Suzie's eyes opened too. The yummy orange smell of the Orange Crush had her head turning towards the pop, and I gave her a drink of her favorite pop. Slowly she drank the whole can of Orange Crush pop though time passed by so quickly. Her trembling cold hand slowly reached up and rested on mine, as she normally did, only that time to tilt my hand to cause the can to tilt. She got her last bit of pop with slurp- pause- slurp sounds.

"Good!' She cheered in her weakened state. Her long fingers gently tapped my knee. I couldn't recall any other time than that we touched so much. Our touch spoke volumes to me, whispers of love, I thought. We made out a list, no words were spoken regarding her decline, only that of favorite food, drinks and sweets that I knew of, rattling them off. Suzie answered by mostly nodding, touching and smiling only a few okays and no's; I had done most of the talking. Some of the items on the list were checked off that day, Suzie seemed to have enjoyed them, but again ate very little. I cried a little throughout our time together that day. I knew

Suzie could hear me, as there was nothing wrong with her ears. I guessed she had just let me have my tears for her, she gave me my privacy. And I was grateful for that as I would have fallen apart. I was sitting on the side of Suzie's bed then because I thought I saw her pat the bed. I was truly a welcome stranger, she didn't know me anymore, at least not as her daughter. But she knew of me in our time together, and I'm sure of it with each passing day that she didn't remember much that it took place. Oh, but there was something there, a connection there, as we lived everyday in the moment, loving each other whether the pat on the bed by her hand was an open invitation or not. It was the three of us together again. Yet I found myself, at a loss for words, it seems like in those times we do find ourselves at a loss for words. Then I remembered a story Suzie loved and thought it quite fitting, so I told it to her the best way I could.

◊

There was a little girl who looked out upon nature, she had been trapped within the confines of her room. Yet, there through her window, she enjoyed nature and its season's change. She was quite fond of autumn and the change it would bring with its cold crisp air; how she loved it there upon her cheek. She would soon see a new life emerge, yet she sometimes would close her eyes, bow her head humbly, and listen to the rustling of the tree's leaves. Then she would open them, raising her head to watch them fall. Some were carried away by the cold autumn breeze, they mumble their goodbyes. But the little girl's interest laid with those that laid below that old Japanese Maple Tree. It adorned with its crimson leaves no more; there they were spread out so elegantly, decorating the earth's floor, there under the Japanese Maple Tree.

◊

How intensely Suzie listened, her blue eyes as wide open as they could be as she placed her hand on my forearm, looking up and into my eyes. I had pause in telling the story. So, she nodded while she squeezed my arm and yes, I continued.

◊

They had become decoration and so much more. How those fallen leaves shuffled about as the cold breeze blew, the little girl heard the whispering sounds of their goodbyes. Their whispers of goodbyes echoed in her mind as they said these hauntingly sad and eternally lovely goodbyes to the tree they once adorned, goodbye to the spring and summer that would be no more. And she (the little girl) said her goodbyes too.

◊

We had both cried, I must have told the story right. Suzie had told it so often over the years, yet I never really paid attention to it until then; there in the nursing home as I sat on Suzie's bed in her decline of life. Suzie had fallen asleep shortly after I had told the tale and I made sure of it- yes, she was asleep. I got up, walking around the room a bit to stretch my legs and too, more so, to gain my composure. I looked at the sign on the bath room door and had a laugh, I did find it quite funny. I then sat in and reclined back on the recliner. Watching Suzie, I had become obsessed with the slight rise and fall of her chest, until I too fell asleep, only to be woken by Kim. "Mrs. Jamie, I thought I heard talking in here a while ago. Visiting hours were over a half hour ago and it is 9: 30 p.m.," Kim informed me in a somewhat irritable tone of voice over such a small matter. I smiled and was quite pleasant to her, which took her off guard, and she in turn had a smile on her face. I was on my way only after looking on Suzie. Kim had stayed in the room watching me as I made my way out, I felt her eyes upon me and it was a pleasant feeling. I looked back at her with a smile, although, I have to admit I thought a frowny face would have been better. But then the thought delivers me from evil as my smile turned into an open mouth smile, and I felt better.

Kim caught up to me past the nurses' station where I stood waiting for the elevator. She gave me the Social Worker's card and informed me that there were two hospice rooms available that Suzie could be moved to then I wouldn't have to leave, I could stay. Then she hugged me telling me how Suzie was one of her favorite patients, and I thanked her for the card. I thanked her for taking care of Suzie, then told her good night and God Bless. She returned the same. Death I thought, would be just that if we kept following our own desires, turning away from the truth, not considering the choices for our action; much more the bigger picture of our lives. I became more than concerned, frightened for myself – for Suzie's soul. I needed to remain in God's love, putting nothing before him, not an easy task. Yet I knew I could do it, with God's help. I thanked God that Jesus gave of himself to the point of death, saving us from sin and its consequences as I was in the elevator going down to the lobby.

I had found myself unable to leave the parking lot, often looking up at the building, wanting to return to Suzie's side. So, I sat in my car and prayed for Suzie. God knew her and I thanked him in Jesus' name for her life. After I had called upon our Lord, I made three calls. I called and had left two messages, one being to the Social Worker in regards to the room change, then the other to Jennifer. I felt bad leaving such a message but knew if I didn't, it would lead to trouble. She would have time to respond to the call before leaving for work in the morning. I knew she checked her messages during her morning coffee and made note of that in the messages. I then called home, apologizing for my lateness, and that I was on my way home, asking if it would be alright that we could talk in the morning. Then I said, "I love you, see you later, Good night and God Bless you," to my husband, and he returned the same.

I drove off, making my way home. This time no music. I was not in the mood. Nor were there memories tugging at my heart, bitter or sweet. I merely felt the need to continue to pray, asking for mercy for my Mom. It was funny, though, I thought about how my Dad would tell me that I had gone to bed with the wants and wake up with the give me. It was so true, and unfortunately, I did most of my talking to God the same way. The request basket full to the point of flowing over if not that. And before I left the car, I gave thanks for the circumstances we were facing- in all things give thanks. It's in the Bible. But by no means did I leave God in the car. No, my hope was to remain in him so he would remain in me – I needed and wanted his love, and knew I was not walking alone, there within those walls a light was on and a silhouette of a man.

I remained there then when my Mom Suzie, my Blue-eyed soul, closed her eyes noting how I would never again see how blue those blue eyes could be.

I remained there then when the funeral director was there to claim the human remains.

I remained, I knew this life was a temporary stay, and I remained in hope that Mom was already at peace and had returned home.

I remained in the elevator, I knew Mom was not there, it was only the three of us. My left hand held onto the stretcher though.

I remained as we stood in the back lot of the nursing home as I continued to hold on to the stretcher watching as the hearse door was opened. Then I heard as he spoke in such a deep, low, calm voice, to tell me to let go. I let go before he pushed the stretcher into the hearse. My body jumped with what I understood to be a slamming sound of the closing of the hearse door. Its sound resonated within me. He had quickly turned to me, hugging me, escorting me to my car. He opened the door and informed me that he would speak with me later, as I got into the car. Closing the car door, I watched him walking to the hearse. I thought if that was me walking there my legs would probably have been like lead. But I noticed his walk seemed to be light as a feather, as if he had no worries, no cares.

I remained following behind the hearse driving out of the back lot; thanking the Lord for Mom's life and loving her.

And I remained as I turned the car to the right as the hearse driver drove straight. I felt removed, yet totally involved. I found myself wiping my sweaty palms on my jeans well. I filled my cheek with air and slowly let it out, then, opening the car window I welcomed in the fresh breeze. I heard a gentle whisper from perhaps the gentle swishing sound from the rustling of the leaves on the trees on that breezy March 11, 2003 evening. I believed I heard her say God was everywhere, Jamie, best you remain.

So many years had passed, so much had changed, and from the world's view I was considered old. It was the Baby Boomers' time to listen to the oldie's music, and I enjoyed listening, yet I thought I was only old in numbers. I referred to myself as a Beloved child of God in labeling, in spirit and in my conduct, with God's help. My hair would be streaked with gray, but I chose to maintain its color and wear it shoulder- length. I believed it helped me look somewhat younger than I was. I hoped it wasn't vain of me, I thought I simply liked the color. Nevertheless, sixteen years had gone by since Mom went home.

My God, time goes by so quickly, and our journey together had its ups and downs, downs by me being distracted in my human frailties. You'd called me back time and time again providing me with wisdom to know better, and courage to speak. And I have spoken the truth about you, about Your glory (not of my own) in everyday life. Yes, I looked back on my life, God, I was not there anymore, and our relationship pressed onward and I glorify you...

And in looking back, memories of loved ones came rushing in there as I sat in my bedroom. Belongings of the present time present in order for the memories not to consume me in my here and now. Yet, here they were, they would come to me: Mom, Raymond, James, Anna, Jennifer and Fred. Just like Dad, he was there too. They all were there in the quietness of silence there in my room. They nudged at me, reminding me of the places they used to be. And I knew the world for me was quieter, colder – void of their warmth, and oh, how I missed the presence of their joy. Then they would slowly leave me, slowly they faded away, all but one. His essence was the strongest, the first to come and always the last to fade away. I could smell his cologne, its fragrance added to the beauty of the sun which then had brighten my room.

I myself adored him, every breath he took; I loved him. I loved him from the top of his head to the tips of his toes, and yes, everything in between. His coming and going I cherished and had eagerly awaited his return. Yes, I adored Fred you see, because he loved me. And I thanked God for him profusely, for he was all I ever wanted here in our physical existence- our gift of life from God. He was second to God and I would miss him until God allowed us to be together again.

I left the comfort of my easy chair, carried on in hope with my day. And I found myself outside near the Japanese Maple tree, its leaves and buds of new life, it was spring. I thought of Mom which led my thoughts to the agony of labor. How wonderful to be a vessel used to bring forth life to the world, I thought. The intense fury of painful contractions of natural birth, muscles that pulled and put pressure upon me. The pain so great only similar to that of several bones being broken at the same time, I'd imagined. All for the pleasure and joy of the first look upon that face- that face. Precious beloved masterpiece from God. Five little fingers on each hand and those ten toes. I wiggled each one of them on both feet! A new touch to feel, a blessing from God. Oh, and that delightful baby smell, awe and that cry; love was there when he was born. I loved him from the top of his head to the tips of his toes. Flesh of our flesh - Fred and mine, my pain was no more. And I thanked God not once but twice for the pain endured, the honor to bring forth life, the pleasure of my boys.

The source of love flowed within the very core of me. Rooted by a supernatural entity who I refer to by his name and eagerly await his return and whose unconditional love rests upon me. I have hungered for it because I knew I was loved from the start. Yes, I adored him, you see, because he first loved me. True God from Ture God begotten not made, of one Being with the Father... Jesus Christ the only Son of God.

What was the point to my life for me, I thought? I sat there beside the maple tree looking out at the beautiful spring sky, breathing in the fresh air of spring in awe of it all. Eventually, I understood that I was not in control of the way I thought I was. But I did have choices. I couldn't force profound change on myself or anyone for that matter. I could, however, create opportunities for change to occur. The change for me was regarding matters of the heart, and God was able to work on that, and did so independently from my effort. It was through that change I was able to do more than survive, more than merely break the vicious cycle of dysfunctional ways to my life. I learned that I was not defined by my past, I wasn't junk. I then could embrace my life's sorrows for understanding, change and closure. Closing doors to the past and living in the moment. Sorrow's woes no longer had a hold on me. I gave thanks to God for my life's experiences and could give thanks and praise him in the midst of all life's circumstances, putting him first was my goal in my everyday life. That isn't easy, meaning everything I would do would have to be to glorify him, not for my own - my life was not my own. And of course, as you know, I could not do it on my own. I would need God's help. And in my journey when I stumbled, when I fell - becoming distracted being human and needing help - I'd turn back to the Lord and he welcomed me home. Likewise, when I turned away, He would call me back with welcome arms. He provides guidance and forgiveness, meeting my needs for change -a relationship with him. For I have changed. I'm in a relationship with him. And I have learned that God's love was/ is and forever would be all inclusive in the absoluteness of everyday life.

Acknowledgments

To the glory of God in my everyday life. Truly God's hand joined to my hand.

To two wonderful guys that have my love. Thanks Alex and Daniel for the understanding and patience, for being my cheerleading team and moreover for their love.

Thank- you to James F. Fitzgerald a visionary, an author, producer and my brother in Jesus Christ. Whose words of wisdom provided me with guidance along the way.

Thank- you to those who supported me Richard Pritts, Jeanette Casciato, Jessica Walter. and Pamela Velez, technical advisor and sister in Christ.

A special thanks to The Rev. Don C. Youse, Jr Vicar of Emmanuel Episcopal Church for his spirituality – steadfast in faith. It has been and will continue to be my pleasure to receive the word through his spirit led unwritten Sunday sermons. And for two of his many reflections Unreasonable Grace and Grace Changes Everything. He continues to create opportunities that strengthen my walk with God. Not to mention, who read and reread the manuscript page after page in the editing process.

Made in the USA
Monee, IL
04 November 2019

16334588R00105